Foolish Of Me

3

Written By:

Allie Marie

Previously

Trinity

I couldn't believe that Kai had just talked to me like that. Yeah, I had a baby by her husband, and I was probably her least favorite person, but I remembered the day of my baby shower when she said she wasn't the kind of woman that would make him choose between her and our son. Kai making a decision not to help me was allowing Mikey to choose between her and MJ. She knew if she told him to be a father, he would. Her word was golden when it came to Mikey. She truly was doing everything out of spite.

Nowadays, it seemed as though I had nobody by my side. The one person who I thought was a friend truly wasn't. No matter how many times I forgave Sharonda, she always let me down.

Only if she had kept giving Kai the medicine to keep her in the coma, I wouldn't have been going through this with Mikey. Sharonda must have thought I was playing when I told her I would give the recording and the video to her job. Well, the joke was on her. I sent the video and recordings to all of the major news outlets. Also, I mailed the video and the recording to the Human Resources department at Penn Hospital.

By this time tomorrow, Sharonda was going to wish she'd never crossed me. The thing that pushed me over the edge was that she always thought she was better than me just because she went to college and became a nurse. She was still the fat bitch that couldn't dress that nobody wanted. She was acting like I told her to drug Kai in the first place, but she was dumb not to believe me when I said I would destroy her if she didn't continue to do as I said.

At this point, I didn't know what to do. I was at my lowest. I literally just asked Kai to help me with Mikey. I needed my mother's love right now the most. These were the times I would ask her what I should do. She really hadn't spoken to me since the day of the baby shower.

I decided to give her a call.

"You have reached the Hughes Family. We are unable to get to the phone right now. Please leave a message at the sanctified beep," my mother's voice came through the phone.

I figured they wouldn't answer. At this moment, all I could do was cry. Maybe this was my karma for sleeping with a married man. All I wanted was to be loved. I personally didn't want Mikey anymore. I just felt like my son shouldn't have to pay for my sins. The sound of my phone vibrating caught my attention. It was my mother. I tried to get myself together to answer the phone, but there was no point. I was at my breaking point.

"Mom..." I sobbed.

"Trinity, what's wrong?"

"Mom, I messed up and I don't know what to do. Mikey wants nothing to do with MJ. All he cares about is his wife, who's currently trying to divorce him. I asked her to talk to him about being there for MJ and she basically treated me like I was shit on the bottom of her shoes. She's no better than me; she's having a baby by another man. All I want is for MJ to have his dad," I explained through my tears.

"Trinity, what did you expect? Did you think his wife was going to help the woman that broke up her marriage? Regardless of her situation, you are the reason for the chain of events that happened in their marriage to crumble. I'm surprised she didn't smack you. I would have," my mom said with nothing but disappointment in her voice. I guess going to Kai was stupid, but she was my last resort.

"I'm desperate. I expected Mikey to be a man and take care of his child. I didn't make him on my own."

"You slept with a married man that you barely knew. All you were to him was a night that was never supposed to happen. I know we don't believe in abortions, but you should have taken that morning-after pill."

"I was giving him something that his wife couldn't."

"Child…" I could tell she was shaking her head at me. "Where did I go wrong with you? Trinity, I'm going to give you some things to think about. Mikey wanted kids; there's no denying that, but he wanted them with his wife. You ever wonder why they didn't seek other options like adoption or being foster parents? It was because he wanted a child with his wife. He didn't just want any child. He wanted a child made out of love in the union of their marriage."

My mom did bring up great points. I never thought about their situation that way, but what was done was done, and I wasn't the blame for our actions resulting in a baby. He should have never taken it there with me that night. Now we had a child to care for, and Mikey needed to do his part as a father.

There was no excuse for his current actions.

"Mom, I see what you're saying, but MJ is here now."

"Exactly, so you have to deal with the consequences of your actions. You had a baby by a man that didn't want to have one by you. The only thing I can advise you to do is to be a good mother to your son. Because my dear, you are a single parent. Just be grateful that Michael helps you out financially. It's some men that don't do anything for their child." She sighed.

She wasn't telling me what I needed to hear. I needed to find a way for Mikey and me to become a family. He couldn't just change the way he was feeling. When Kai was in the coma, I finally had the relationship I wanted. MJ finally had his father full-time. The only problem I saw in this equation was Kai. I felt like she was a puppet master, and Mikey was her puppet. She had all the control over him and his heart.

"Trinity, you need to come back to church. You need God in your life."

"After you and my father shunned me? I think not!"

"God didn't turn his back on you. Just think about it. I'm going to let you go. Kiss my grandson for me. Maybe one day we can have you over for dinner," she stated like I was just a guest and not her daughter. She literally felt the need to say maybe sometime in the future, I would be welcome back into their home. My own parents home!

"Whatever," I mumbled before hanging up.

Looking up at the clock, I couldn't believe I was in the parking lot for almost two hours. I had to get back to Sharonda. She was watching MJ for me. I knew that was real shady of me to ask her to watch my son while I went out to destroy her life, but oh well. I just needed to get to her before her job called her.

Taking my car out of park, I saw a crying Kai walking in my direction. What did this bitch have to cry about? She had two men loving her who wanted to be her child's father. These men were falling at her feet, ready to give her the world, but here she was, crying, while my son was becoming another statistic as a fatherless child. My body filled with anger as I watched her continue to her car, not looking at her surroundings.

You're dumb as hell if you think I'm going to help you with anything.

Kai's words kept running through my head as I put my car in drive. If she wouldn't help, then the only thing I could think of was eliminating the problem. Pushing on the gas pedal, I ran straight into her. All I could see was her body flying up into the air and landing on the top of my car.

"Oh my God!" I screamed as reality set in. "I really hit her..." I heard her groaning as she lay on the top of the car.

"Hey!" I heard someone yelling.

"Fuck," I mumbled. Pulling off, all I could see out my rear-view mirror was Kai's body rolling off my car and landing on the ground.

Chapter 1

Trinity

"**F**uck! Fuck! Fuck!" I screamed as I sped away in my car. I couldn't believe I'd just hit Kai. My mind was racing as I broke every traffic law to get to Sharonda's house. When I pulled off, I knew Kai was still alive because I heard her moaning and groaning in pain. For her child, who knows? It was sad to say but I hope it dies so Mikey could come to his senses. But then again, I knew had he ever found out I did this he would probably try to kill me.

Pulling up to Sharonda's house, I looked in the mirror. I didn't even realize I had blood pouring from a gash in my head. I tried to clean it up as much as I could before getting out of the car and knocking on her door.

"You're back so soon? I thought I was going to have my god baby with me all day." Sharonda pouted, allowing me to walk into her house.

"No, we have to get going," I replied back as I looked around for his diaper bag. I didn't know where I was going but I knew I had to leave the state of Pennsylvania.

"Trinity, what happened to your face?" Sharonda asked me with much concern dripping from her voice.

"I was in a little fender bender on my way to your house," I quickly lied. There was no way I was telling her the truth, especially since I had just probably ruined her career and she could possibly be facing jail time.

"You probably need some stitches. Do you want me to take you to the hospital."

"No!" I yelled unintentionally. "No, I have to get going."

"Okay let me get MJ ready. You should have called. I would have had him prepared," Sharonda then stressed while walking up the stairs.

I paced the living room trying to think of my next move. I knew I couldn't go on the run with my baby. All MJ would do is slow me down. So I had to think of something. I didn't have any money but what Mikey gives me a month, which was only a thousand dollars a month. I wasn't going to survive with that money. Plus, I needed a new car. There was no way I could continue to ride around in mine.

One, because I was pretty sure the police had a description of it; probably even my license plate. And two, Kai banged it up pretty bad, causing it to look like I was in a hit and run.

"Alright, big boy is all ready?" Sharonda came down the steps with my handsome son in tow. "Since you don't want to go to the hospital let me clean and stitch up this wound. I would hate for you to get an infection."

"Okay," I agreed. I started to feel like shit because Sharonda was a good person. She honestly was my only friend and I just allowed my anger to get her into some serious trouble. If I could turn back the hands of time, I would have never sent in those videotapes. Now seeing that my life is spiraling out of control, I wished I would have accepted my fate.

How foolish of me to fight for a man that was never mine to begin with?

"Keep that area dry and within a week go to the doctors to have the stitches taken out."

"Thanks."

"No problem," she said and then walked over to make sure MJ was buckled up." I'm going to take him to the car for you. You look like you're in pain. I really wish you would go to the hospital."

I waved her over. "I'm okay... I promise."

"Damn, what did you hit? The roof of your car is damn near caved in." By now, we were headed to my car when Sharonda asked that, causing me to look at it. It looked bad. I had to get out of open with this car.

"I done hit a damn deer on my way here. I'm just happy MJ wasn't in the car with me. I'm headed to drop him off to Mikey's parents' house now then take my car to the shop."

"Okay be safe. Let me know when you get home." She said as I put MJ in the car.

"I will... Sharonda," I called her name, stopping her from opening her front door. "I just want to let you know I'm sorry for all of the things I did to you. You're really a good friend."

"Awwww thanks bestie. It's cool you know we always fight and make up it's no problem." She said before walking in the house. I knew this would be the last time that I would talk to her.

Next stop was Mama Bullock's house. It was time for them to step up since Mikey didn't want to be a father. They needed to help. This was a hard decision to make because I loved my son. However, I knew traveling on the road with him wasn't good. He needed a stable environment. Hopefully with me dropping MJ off they will force Mikey to become the father he needs to be.

"Baby, mommy loves you. I love you so much I did the unthinkable. MJ, I just wanted to give you the best life I could. I promise when I'm settled I will send for you." I rambled on to him. Looking back, tears began to fall. I couldn't believe I'd allowed myself to do this. Committing crimes was not me, and I knew I will never survive jail.

"Hey, Trinity, it's a bad time," Mama Bullock said in a rushed tone. She was already rushing out of the house with Grandma Lucy and Papa Bullock on her heels.

"I'm sorry, but I need help."

"Okay, give me a call. We're on our way to the hospital. Kai was involved in a hit and run." I felt like my heart stop. *How did they know?*

"Oh, that's sad. Do they know who did that to her?"

"No, some maniac driving out the parking lot. But she's in labor and we need to be there to support Mikey. He's not allowed near her due to the restraining order she has on him." Hearing them say they're running to support Kai and Mikey made me beyond pissed. So piss that it started to take away the guilt of hitting her. I hope her and that bastard dies.

"Well, I came here because I need a break. MJ needs to spend some time with Mikey or his family. I can't continue to do this by myself." I was damn near having a nervous breakdown.

"Little girl, this is not the time. Your problem is with Mikey. That is yall child! We done raised ours so do what you need to do." Grandma Lucy had to add her two cents.

"I don't know why yall are running to Kai's aid and her baby's not even Mikey's. I heard her say it herself. Mikey is just in denial. So I'm going to tell you what I'm going to do—"

"You're getting beside yourself." Mama Bullock snapped. I didn't have time to go back and forth with them. I placed MJ's car seat on their front step along with his diaper bag and ran to my car. I had to get the fuck out of here.

"Trinity, what are you doing? What happen to your car?" I heard Papa Bullock yelling behind me. I didn't have time to explain. Sooner or later, everyone would know what I had done. I knew Kai saw when I hit her. She looked me right in the eyes. Now I just have to find a way for my parents to give me some money and ditch this car. They were my last hope to get out of this mess I'd created.

Chapter 2

Quadir

I barely parked the car before hopping out. Ava had just called me telling me that Kai was involved in a hit and run accident. The whole way to the Jefferson Hospital, I prayed. I swear baby girl couldn't win for losing. Walking to the front entrance of the hospital I spotted Mikey's bitch ass standing outside the emergency door, crying his fucking heart out. Seeing him there only pissed me off farther. I blamed him for this shit happening. If he had just signed the divorce papers she wouldn't have even been in that parking lot in the first place.

"Don't do it." Majesty said when he saw me walking in Mikey's direction. I forgot I was with him when Ava called. "Go see ya daughter be born."

"I swear it's only a matter of time before I put a bullet in his head." I mumbled running inside the hospital and going to the front desk. "Excuse me, my girl was rushed in here. Her name is Kai Rose-Bullock. She's pregnant and she was involved in a hit and run."

"Yes, are you dad?"

"Yeah," I said as she did something on the computer. "She's in labor and delivery. Room 225."

"Quadir! Quadir!" Ava yelled, walking toward me.

"Come on. All she keeps doing is asking for you. She won't push without you in the room." Hearing that she about to have my baby had me scared out of my mind. Kai wasn't full term. She was only thirty-two weeks.

Ava directed Majesty and me to the elevators that led to labor and delivery.

"Kai they need you to push," I heard Ms. Dana yell.

"Call Quadir. I'm not having this baby without him! My baby's not ready to be here." Kai screamed as I walked in the room. Inside were my mom and Ms. Dana.

"Mrs. Bullock, you have to push. The baby is losing oxygen," the doctor stated, trying to get her to understand.

"Kai, I'm here. Please baby push. Do whatever they ask you to do." I said walking to her side and grabbing her hand. She had tears running down her face, and I could see the fear all over it. Even though I was feeling the same thing, I knew I had to be strong for her and my baby. "We're good baby and so is our daughter. Just calm down and push." I instructed as my mom and Ms. Dana held both of her legs.

"Kai, we need you to push on the count of three. One, Two, Three push as hard as you can." The doctor said. I watch Kai bare down and push.

"Ahhhh…." she screamed.

"What's wrong?" I asked in a panic, like a dummy, causing everybody to look at me with the death stare.

"She is doing this natural. No epidural." My mom said. Than started to coach Kai to continue pushing.

"You're doing good Kai. I see the baby's head. All we need is another big push and she will be out." The doctor added.

I wiped the sweat beads that were forming on her head while whispering encouraging words in her ear. After this experience, I swear I was looking at women differently. I didn't even know how Kai was enduring this after being hit by a car. Just looking at her I could tell she was banged up. She had some bruises starting to form on her arms and legs and I could just imagine what the rest of her body looked like.

"Alright, One, Two, Three." Kai squeezed my hand so hard I wanted to slap her upside her head. I just knew my hand was fractured.

"She's coming," Ms. Dana announce with tears in her eyes. "Keep pushing Kai."

"I'm trying," Kai cried out. Her honey light skin was as red as a tomato as she gave another push.

After that one push, the doctor announced, "You have a baby girl."

"Why isn't she crying?" Kai asked and my heart dropped because I didn't hear a cry either. I watched as multiple doctors came rushing in the delivery room, and place my baby in an incubator. I then rushed over to look at her while taking my phone out and snapped a quick picture.

"She did cry. It was faint," Ms. Dana held a crying Kai." Baby, calm down. They already told you that this was going to happen."

"What was going to happen?" I began to panic as they rolled my daughter out of the room.

"Quadir, they're taking the baby to the NIC- Unit. She's premature and they advised us that when the baby is delivered they were immediately taking her to the NIC- Unit to stabilize her and make sure she's okay."

"I didn't get to see or hold her." Kai whispered.

"We will." I handed her the phone to see the picture I was able to take, while praying to God that my baby girl made it. I was already going on a killing spree. Kai was the most loving and caring person in the world but it seemed like pain and harm seemed to follow her, and I didn't like that. "Babe do you know who did this to you?"

"Yeah," she responded barely above a whisper.

"Who was it?"

"Quadir, promise me you won't do anything crazy."

"Kai who was it?" I asked again. I wasn't trying to hear anything she was spitting. I know whoever did this tried to kill her and made my baby come into the world prematurely. Now my daughter fighting for her life. Somebody was going to die. This was one promise that I would have to break.

"I won't."

"It was Trinity! She's the one who hit me."

"That bitch!" Ms. Dana said before storming out the room.

"Please get my mom. I know Mikey's family is here." I swear I couldn't get rid of Mikey soon enough. Not only did he cheat on her and wouldn't give her the divorce, but he had his dumb ass babymama trying to kill her. "One of you please gets my mom."

"I'll be right back." I kissed her before walking out the room. All I could hear was screaming. Walking into the waiting room, Mr. August was holding Ms. Dana back from some lady in an old ass wig. I notice Mikey's Grandma Lucy sitting over in the corner shaking her head.

I asked, "What's going on here?"

"All we want to do is be supportive of Kai. She just had our grandchild! Regardless of them going through a divorce, we are still going to be a part of the baby's life."

"No the fuck you're not! Grandma Lucy can because I fuck with her. But yall muthafuckas ain't going anywhere near my child." I snapped. I was over this bullshit.

"How are you so sure the baby is yours? She is still married to my son!" Mikey's father asked in a matter of fact tone. I wanted to punch that nigga in his face.

"Yall just as delusional as your dumb ass son. Kai has been telling your son that this baby is not his. The only baby he has is by that dead bitch walking when I get my hands on her." Ms. Dana explained.

"Whatever! We want a DNA test? Yall will not keep us away if that baby is my son's. I will fight for grandparent's rights if I have too."

"Mary," Grandma Lucy said. "Let's go!"

"Your son doesn't even take care of the child he has now. The only grandparent's right you have is to the fucking baby in your mother's arms. Especially since his mother is about to go to jail. That crazy bitch hit my daughter! Now yall want to come up here adding insult to injury. Your son and family caused enough pain." Ms. Dana cried. That's how angry she was.

"Where is his babymama?" Majesty asked walking up to us. I already knew he was putting a plan in motion to find this bitch.

"We don't know," Mary said, to quick for my liking, but the looking her husband face look like they knew otherwise.

"What's her name?" He asked.

"Why what are you going to do? You're not the police." Mikey's father said. "She has a child to live for." That was it. I straight two pieced him. Dropping him where he stood only for Mr. August to start stomping him.

"What the fuck you mean she has a child to live for? So my daughter and granddaughter life doesn't matter?" Mr. August roared.

"Please stop!" Mary screamed as hospital security started running toward the commotion. Majesty put his hand up, dismissively, and they turned around. I could see why Mikey's bitch ass couldn't fight, neither could his father. He didn't even try to fight back. All he did was curl his body up into a ball.

"What's her name?"

"Her name is Trinity Hughes." Grandma Lucy responded than walked out of the hospital with Mikey's son in her arms.

"That's all I needed." Majesty said before dapping me up. "I'll find her."

"Don't kill her I want to do that." I whispered. I couldn't wait to wrap my hand around Trinity's throat and feel like life slip from her body.

"What the fuck are yall still here? Yall are not family. Does she need to get a restraining order on you too?" Ms. Dana snapped at Mikey parents. They finally took the hint and made their way to the exit.

"Mom, calm down." Ava said dialing someone on her phone. "Have anybody heard from Aubrey? I keep calling her and its going straight to voicemail."

"No." Mr. August answered, pacing back and forth.

"My Aunt Rita is on her way to the hospital with Kylie and Rashawn," Nasir let us know, walking up to us. "Congrats bro."

"Thanks." It had just hit me that I was a father. I'd never have been so happy in my life. She was beautiful and so small. I had never known I could love someone so fast, and I was going to give baby girl the world. I was ready to give Kai the world too. Without her, I would've never been able to experience this. Our relationship was moving so fast but I didn't regret a moment with her.

"I'm going to go back into the room with Kai," I mentioned before walking away from the family. I swear nothing could bring down my joy. I walked into Kai's room to find her still crying.

"Babe, stop crying. Our baby is going to be good. She's a fighter just like you." I swear Kai had nine lives. She survived being shot, now hit by a car.

"Quadir, I need you to take a DNA test," she mumbled, but I heard her perfectly clear. All I knew was, she better had explained herself before her ass ended up missing, just like Trinity was about to.

Chapter 3

Kai

"**W**hat the fuck you mean I need to take a DNA test?" Quadir barked, causing me to jump from the boominess of his voice. The look in his eyes had me ready to shit bricks. It was like he had transformed into a different person right in front of me.

"Ummm..." I couldn't understand why my words were stuck in the back of my throat.

"Kai, you have ten seconds to tell me why I need a DNA test. Is there something I need to know? Let me know now."

"No... It's just that the judge didn't want to grant my divorce right then and there because Mikey kept claiming that the baby was his. So the judge didn't grant it because a custody agreement would have to set in place."

"Damn, Kai, why ya big headed ass didn't say that to begin with instead of having me thinking of ways to murder you in my head?" He said with a smirk, but his eyes told me he was dead serious.

"You're crazy," I mumbled.

"Yeah, but you stuck with me now!" He shot back before the door opened and the doctors walked in. The look on their faces had me wanting to cry. I had no idea what to expect.

"My name is Dr. Roberts and I'm the head physician of the NIC –Unit." He said, holding out his hand. Quadir stood up and shook it. The doctor then walked over to me to shake mine. "What's the baby name?"

"Miracle," I answered, looking at Quadir to see if he would object or not—which he didn't. I felt like that was the best name to give her because she was my miracle. This pregnancy was hard and tough. Not only did she survive me being shot, but she survived me being stressed and now me getting hit by a car. On top of all that, she was now fighting to stay alive, but I knew this was a battle that she would win.

"So as you know, Miracle is only thirty two weeks. She weighs three pounds and eight ounces. Premature babies can survive being born this early, and she is doing very well under the circumstances. She is breathing on her own. We put a feeding tube through her nose so she can begin eating. Mom we need you to start pumping breast milk is what best for her. If you choose not to pump we have some consent forms asking if we can give the baby donor breast milk."

"No, I will pump. I planned on breast feeding any way."

"Great. Now I have to let you be aware of these things that can happen to Miracle. Being as though Miracle is premature she is at risk of having cerebral palsy. There's a chance of her being blind and or deaf. With premature babies they do not always develop as fast as a baby born full term. I'm not saying this will happen to Miracle but I just have to let you know the chances. Now if we discover she has some kind of problem. We have wonderful resources to help handicap children."

All I could do was break down in cry. I had never caused any harm to anyone. Never had wished ill on anyone, but it seemed like no matter what, I just couldn't catch a break. My heart was breaking thinking about all of the challenges Miracle might have face, all because of some crazy bitch that couldn't get out of her feelings. I had no idea why Trinity would think trying to kill me would solve her problems. Mikey did not want her or their child, and that had nothing to do with me.

No matter what she thought, Mikey just didn't want to be a father to MJ.

"Kai, Miracle's going to be good. He just have to tell us this to prepare us, but even if something is wrong, we're not going to love her any less. So, stop crying. She needs us to be strong for her. Nothing but positive energy." Quadir said, wiping my tears. And he was right. God had the last say in this. I always been a praying woman and I was going to continue to pray for my daughter's health.

"When can we see her?"

"Right now, I just want Nurse Jackie here to teach you how to use the breast pump. We want to get you on a schedule. After that mom and dad, you are able to go in the NIC-Unit to see your precious baby girl." Doctor Roberts said before walking out. After fifteen minutes of learning to pump, they put me on an every four hour regiment and we were ready to see Miracle.

When we walked into the NIC –Unit everyone was sweet and nice. They were understanding and compassionate. That was everything that I need at this moment, because I didn't know if I could accept any more bad news.

"Congratulation mom and dad. She's beautiful. My name is Rebecca and I will be her nurse for tonight. One thing that I like to suggest to the parents is our kangaroo technique. Kangaroo care is a technique where the premature baby is placed in an upright position on its mother's bare chest, allowing tummy-to-tummy contact that positions the baby between the mother's breasts. The baby's head is turned so that its ear is positioned above the mother's heart. Dad can do it also. It helps your baby maintain its body warmth and have a better chance of successful breastfeeding. Kangaroo care has emotional benefits for you, too. It builds your confidence and reduces your stress as you provide intimate care that can improve your baby's health and well-being."

"Thank you. We definitely want to do that." I said smiling.

"So, mom, are you ready to hold Miracle? Honestly she's doing great. She's breathing on her own and that's awesome. Right now, all it seems we have to do is fatten her up and she is out of here before you know it."

"Yes, I'm ready to hold her." I couldn't contain my excitement. Rebecca walked us over to the incubator. Miracle was beautiful with a head full of curly black hair. She was sleeping so peacefully that I didn't even want to disturb her.

"Are we doing the kangaroo technique this time?" Rebecca inquired and I shook my head yes.

"Let me get you a screen to cover this section so you will have privacy." She suggested before walking away.

"Sir, we need you to take a step outside with us." Another nurse, that was a man, came tapping Quadir on his shoulder.

"Why?" Quadir asked, looking him up and down. I could feel this was about to be some bullshit. The nurse looked like he was just put in a bad situation.

"The police are asking for you."

What the hell? I thought. What else could be possibly happening right now? I tried to get up out of the wheel chair to see what's going on, but Quadir put a stop to that.

"Kai sit down!"

"No, I need to see what's going on. You didn't do anything. We just had our daughter. What else could go wrong I can't take this." I cried out.

"I'm sure it's nothing. I'll be right back." With that, Quadir walked off, towards the exit. It was at the same time Rebecca came back with her smiling face.

"Mom, are you ready?" She asked me.

"Can you please roll me outside the door real quick? I want to let my boyfriend know we're about to hold our baby."

"Sure." She smiled and started to push me towards the automatic door leading out to the hallway. The sight in front of me would have brought me to my knees if I weren't already sitting in the wheel chair. There were four police officers and they had Quadir on the ground with his hands behind his back, arresting him.

"Wait... What are you doing?" I shouted, causing Quadir to look at me.

"Kai, it's okay. Just go back inside the room. I'll be back before you know it." Quadir tried assuring me before turning his head away from me.

"Quadir Muhammad, you being arrested for the physical assault of Michael Bullock. You have the right to remain silent. Anything you say can and will be used against you in a court of law. You have the right to an attorney. If you cannot afford an attorney, one will be provided for you. Do you understand the rights I have just read to you?" That was one of the officers reading Quadir his rights.

Just hearing them pained me more.

"Yeah, muthafucka, just hurry up and take me to the precinct," Quadir snapped as they picked him up and started walking him down the hall.

"Why God?" I screamed and broke down crying. Everything in my life was crumbling down, and it was all because of Mikey.

"Kai, you're a strong woman. You will get through this." Rebecca said, trying to comfort me. Her words fell on death ears as I watched the love of my life and father of my child get hauled off to jail, because of my husband.

Chapter 4

Amber

I'd been calling Rashawn's phone for the last couple of hours and he hadn't answered yet. Every one of my calls was going straight to the voicemail. And it was pissing me off. I don't what I have to do to get in contact with him. I was so desperate that I was ready to burn this house down just to send a smoke signal.

Right now, I had Aubrey and her little boyfriend tied up to her dining room chairs. I couldn't believe the audacity of this bitch to keep talking shit after I'd already shot her. Granted, it was just a flesh wound, but this bitch's mouth was going to cause me to kill her prematurely. I'd given myself the grand tour of their home and I hated to admit, I quite jealous. I did notice that none of Rashawn's clothes was in the master bedroom. So maybe she wasn't lying about her and Rashawn not being together for the time being. But, I knew Rashawn, and he would never allow her to be with anyone else. Not and live a peaceful life.

"Ayo, crazy!" Aubrey called out to me, laughing.

"What did I tell you about calling me crazy, bitch?" I screamed, walking up to her and punching her in the face. It felt good beating on her, especially since I knew she couldn't defend herself.

"Fuck you!" She spit the blood from her mouth in my face. "You're the dumbest bitch I have ever met. You're seriously calling Rashawn from your phone. He doesn't answer numbers he doesn't know on his personal cell, dickhead. Meanwhile, while your Cynthia doll looking ass from Rugrats pulling out the little bit of hair you have left, Rashawn has been blowing up my damn phone!"

I looked at her phone and it had sixteen missed calls from an Ava, Rashawn, her mother and Ms. Rita. I didn't know why everybody was blowing her up, but it must've been serious. I then went to her text messages. I went to Rashawn's first and I could see him begging, asking her for forgiveness and all of his messages went unanswered. Who the fuck this bitch thought she was, God's gift to men? She was talking about her worth and how she felt she deserved better than him.

I wasn't going to lie; it made me feel better knowing he'd probably dogged her the way he'd done me.

"How does it feel to know Rashawn's not shit?" I wanted to taunt her. She swore she was everything Rashawn ever wanted and needed, but from what I'd gathered from their texts was that he'd been cheating on her. It felt good knowing she was probably knocked off her little pedal stool.

"I'm obviously handling it better than ya retarded ass. I'm not out here getting abortions and shooting up wedding parties."

"Umm, are you going to call somebody or just have us tied up for no reason?'" Morgan asked, and I just looked at him. Poor thing didn't even know he probably was about to die, and not by my hands. Once Rashawn found out about him it was going to be lights out.

"Morgan, right? You should enjoy the time you have left being alive. You don't know what you even got yourself into, dealing with this hoe."

"Who supposed to kill me? You...her babydad?" He asked, chuckling. The fear I saw in his eyes before was gone. He now looked annoyed by my antics.

"Oh, he must not know Rashawn? Aubrey, let him know my husband, your fiancée, isn't wrapped too tight." Just as the words left my mouth, Aubrey looked at me like I was getting on her last nerves.

"I'm not worried about a man that's stupid enough to not see the Queen in front of him. Plus no nigga put fear in my heart. I don't give a fuck who he is!" He sounded so confident, and from the look on Aubrey face it look like she liked his answer.

"We'll see."

"Bitch..." was all Aubrey said before her phone started ringing. And look and behold, it was Rashawn. I answered it then put it on speaker.

"Yo' Aubrey, why the fuck you not answering ya fucking phone?" Rashawn barked before I could say hello.

"That's because she's a little tied up right now," I explained, laughing.

"Amber?"

"Yes, hubby it's me, the one and only. Come on home. I miss you. We have a lot to discuss, especially about your precious little fiancée and her side nigga." I laughed, knowing what I'd just said had him heated.

"Her side nigga? I see everybody wants to die tonight, huh?" He roared. "Put her ass on the phone!"

"Nope! I'll see you in a few, baby," I laughed before hanging up in his face. I'd just informed him that I had his bitch hostage and all he heard was the part about her side nigga. "I guess he really don't care about your safety."

"Amber, please, you know and so does he that the only reason he's coming is for me. Don't play yourself!" Aubrey shouted. I didn't even care that she was telling the truth. My mission was accomplished. Rashawn was on his way over and I had to get ready. I saw some new lingerie with the tag still on them in her closet. I was about to be on my grown and sexy to show this nigga what he was missing, but not before I ducked taped her and Morgan's mouth shut.

Chapter 5

Rashawn

"Yo," I called out to Nasir, waving him over. He looked to be having a real intense conversation with Ava. I knew Ava hadn't really been feeling him since Kari yelled out to the whole barbershop that she was pregnant.

"Wassup?" Nasir said, shaking his head. I could see the stress lines forming on his forehead.

"Amber is at the house with Aubrey," I stated, causing his eyes to buck.

"What the fuck are you still doing here?" He snapped.

"I'm about to leave. I'm telling you now, you might as well get my bail money together. She was talking crazy about Aubrey and her side nigga at my house." I was fuming. Not only did Aubrey think she broke up with me, but she was disrespecting me as well by having some nigga up in the house I was still paying all of the bills at. The way I was feeling, it was about to be three bodies dropping tonight.

"Rashawn, you focused on the wrong shit. Go get my sis and take care of Amber," Nasir voice as the elevator doors open.

"Yo, what the fuck yall doing?" I barked as I watch four police officers escorting Quadir towards the exit.

"Ava, go to the NIC-Unit with Kai," was all Quadir said before looking at Nasir. I hated that twin shit. Ever since we were little they had their own communication. It was like they knew what the other was thinking. The shit was weird. These niggas would just bust out laughing at the same time without even looking at each other. They we're so in sync that if one of them caught a bad vibe from someone, without even saying a word, the other was T'ing off on the nigga with no question asked.

"I'm about to meet him at the precinct. Take care of Amber! There are no excuses! I'm telling you now, if you don't, Quadir will, and her death is going to be a slow one. If you can't, just keep her put until Quadir can come take care of her," Nasir ranted.

"Nigga, I'm going to take care of Amber!" I was offended for the simple fact that this nigga stood in my face and doubted the capability of my trigger finger. What he needed to worry about was if I was stable enough to wait out Kari's pregnancy before I put a bullet in her head.

"Yeah, alright," Nasir said, brushing me off before jogging towards the exit.

Everything was getting out of control. Amber had done reared her ugly head, Aubrey on some bullshit and Kai couldn't catch a damn break. I can't wait until shit got back to normal.

Aubrey really hadn't been feeling me since the whole Cinnamon situation. We barely talked. We only communicated if it had something to do with Kylie. Other than that, she didn't want anything to do with me. Then on top of all that, my relationship with Nasir had been strained. He knew I was ready to body Kari's snake ass for trying to blackmail me. The only thing that was stopping me was because she supposedly had been pregnant with that dickhead's baby.

All I had to say about that was, he better had got right with Ava because Amari and his new jit was about to be a motherless child.

When I pulled up to the house, all the lights were out. *Fuck,* I mumbled. Pulling out my keys, I realized Aubrey dumb ass had changed the fucking locks on me. See, this happened when you trying to be smart. Now she stuck in the damn house with a fucking psycho. Walking up to the door, I turned the handle and just my luck it was unlocked.

"I've been waiting for you," Amber announced when I walked inside. She was walking down the steps with her gun pointed at me. Looking around, I didn't see Aubrey or her so called side nigga in sight. Amber had candles lit all around the house and the peddles from the roses I had delivered making a path from the front door to the steps.

I didn't know if I should've been nervous, pissed, or concerned. Amber had on one of the *"I'm sorry"* gifts that I'd sent Aubrey. It was a see through teddy lingerie and thong set from Nordstrom's. She had her hair out, and it wasn't the long black silky hair I used to love running my fingers through. Baby girl had multiple bald spots in her head now. Her smooth vanilla skin looked gray and the lingerie was falling off of her due to the massive weight loss.

"Amber, put the gun away," I finally told her after taking in the whole scene in front of me.

"No! I'm not dumb Rashawn! You just want me to put it down so you can kill me." Amber then walked up to me smiling. I swear I wanted to throw up as soon as I smelled her breath. Looking at her rotten teeth I could see why her breath wasn't up to par. "Nope not going to happen," she taunted, trying to wrap her arms around me but I pushed her back, causing the smile to wipe off her face.

"Where's Aubrey?"

"Why are you asking for her?" Amber screamed, now pacing back and forth.

"What the fuck you mean why I'm asking for her? I called her and your crazy ass answered, talking about you holding my girl hostage."

"Rashawn, you know I hate that word," she yelled, hitting herself with the butt of the gun like it was calming her down.

"Amber, what do you want from me?" I genuinely asked. I really needed to know. Seeing her like this was tugging a nigga's heart. I never imagine Amber would turn out like this. It was fucked up, because I knew I had to kill her. I knew there was no way she would just leave, and leave my family and me alone.

Amber then looked me in the eyes and smiled weakly.

"All I ever wanted from you was love. That's all I wanted! And all you did was do me dirty. You dogged me out so bad that I thought I wasn't worth love. I had someone who loved me but I couldn't return the love because all I ever wanted was you. Why couldn't you see that I was enough?" She cried out to me.

"Amber..." I started but she cut me off.

"I killed Jalisa and boy did I enjoy it. I can still hear her screams in my head." Her eyes turned cold and she let out a wicked chuckle. Amber had completely lost her mind.

"Where's Aubrey?" I asked again. I just wanted to make sure she was safe. I wouldn't have been able to forgive myself had something happened to her. I was supposed to have found Amber a long time ago, but I had been bullshitting. So, if anything happened to her it would've been my fault.

"She's all you care about!" Amber screamed. "She's out here fucking other men! I never strayed from you. I was always loyal and faithful to you!" Without notice, she turned around and made a dash towards the dining room. I ran after her and stopped when she was standing behind beat up Aubrey. I looked around quickly to see if anyone else was in the room but Aubrey was here by herself. I couldn't tell if Aubrey was scared or mad, but seeing her beat up had me pissed.

"Amber, put the fucking gun down! We're not even together so you holding Aubrey hostage and beating her is for nothing," I barked, moving closer to her. I knew if I pulled my gun out it would've be over for Aubrey. Amber would've killed her without a doubt.

"I don't care if yall together or not. I don't like this bitch! She is the main reason why you didn't want to be with me when you got out of jail. I wasted my life holding you down and as soon as you got out and found this hoe and ya bastard, it was fuck Amber, right?" Amber had tears falling from her eyes. I hated that she believed things was more than they really were. However, I never lied to her. Amber knew for a fact that I was never going to be with her.

Was I wrong for not stopping the whole situation while I was in prison because I knew her feelings were deeper than mine? *Yes.* I took full responsibility for that.

"Just kill the bitch, now!" Aubrey groaned, looking at me. Amber yanked her head back by her hair. With one swift motion, I pulled my gun out but before I could shoot, I saw Amber head yank back and a nigga came and slit her throat with Aubrey's butcher knife.

"Who the fuck is this nigga?" I barked as Amber's body fell to the floor, making gargling noises as she tried the breathe. One, he killed Amber and she was my kill. Secondly, Aubrey did have some nigga up in my crib. They both ignored me as he continued to cut the bandage that was tied around Aubrey's hands and feet. As soon as Aubrey was release she fell in the nigga's arms like he was her knight in shining armor. Pulling them apart, I pistol whipped this nigga and gripped Aubrey up.

"What are you doing?" She cried. I wanted to feel bad for putting my hands on her. Especially since Amber had already fucked her up. But looking at her in the arms of another nigga had me ready to call the clean-up crew to clean up three bodies instead of one. I could hear the nigga moaning and groaning as he tried to get up. I know my blow to his head had him a little daze.

"Aubrey, I'm only going to ask you this one time," I stated in a calm voice. I knew my voice might have been calmed, but I was everything but calm on the inside.

"Morgan," she finally whispered.

"This is Morgan? The same muthafucka I questioned you about?" I remembered her goofy ass smiling hard as shit in her phone during the New Year's Eve party. She told me he was a fucking co-worker. I didn't think much of it because he did have a bitch's name.

"Listen…" was all she could get out before I threw her down on the floor and made my way to Morgan. Gripping this nigga up and him pushing me right back off of him only caused me to punch him right in the face. He stumbled back, tripping over Amber's dead body. As soon as his body hit the floor, I sent a kick to his face. I could hear his jaw crack. I didn't know if Aubrey thought I was playing or not, but she was about to be the cause of this man's death. I'd told her multiple times not to fuck with me.

"Oh my God! Please stop. You're going to kill him," I heard her scream but her pleads fell on deaf ears. I didn't stop until I felt myself being pulled away. Turning around, it was Rome pulling me out of the dining room and I saw a frighten Tika holding a crying Aubrey.

"Yo, what the fuck is your problem?" Rome snapped at me like I was losing my mind. Morgan was barely conscious.

"Morgan, I'm so sorry." Aubrey sobbed, trying to climb over to Morgan. Her actions were only pissing me off more.

"Aubrey, don't touch him!" I shouted, pointing my gun at her.

"Rashawn, no!" Tika begged, pulling Aubrey away from Morgan. "Babe, we have to get him to the hospital." Tika then said to Rome with pleading eyes. Rome let out a sigh, knowing I was against getting that nigga any help.

"Naw. Aubrey knew what the fuck was going to happen. I warned her stubborn ass one to many times. Do you take me for a fucking joke?" I barked at Aubrey who only cried harder.

"Please, he saved my life!" Aubrey screamed back to me. "Rashawn, if you want me to be back with you fine. I'm willing to make our relationship work. Please, just help him!"

I let out an evil chuckle. Aubrey must've been out of her rabbit ass mind if she thought I was going to allow this nigga to live and breathe the same breath that he would use to tell people that he had my girl. Rome was giving me a look but I didn't know what the fuck he wanted me to do.

"Man, he saved Aubrey. Just call Doc to check him out. I can promise you that this nigga not fucking with Aubrey anymore after this. Plus, the doctor need to come anyway to check Aubrey face out." Rome suggested. He had a point. This nigga was kidnapped held hostage by a psycho for a couple hours then got his ass beat after he wanted to play superhero. Any person in their right frame of mind could see Aubrey came with too much bullshit.

"Please, Rashawn," Aubrey begged. All her begging for this nigga's health was only making me regret not shooting him.

"How the fuck yall know what was going on here?" I asked. It had just dawned on me that Rome and Tika just popped up out of the blue.

"Tika been trying to reach Aubrey because she knew she went out or some shit like that, and she got worried when Aubrey didn't call her to let her know she was in the house. So she broke down and told me the sneaky shit they's been up too." Rome explained, shaking his head at his wife. All I could do was laugh because Tika and Aubrey were in cahoots with one another with all this sneaking around.

"Alright," I mumbled, hating the fact that I was about to help this nigga but I had to admit, he did save Aubrey's life. I was sure Amber was going to kill her and it wasn't a guarantee that my bullet would have killed Amber before she pulled her own trigger. "Make the calls to the clean-up crew and the doc."

Aubrey let out a sigh of relief. She was still crying but I know she knew not to fuck with me. I meant what I said, the only reason why this nigga was living to see another day was because he saved her life.

Letting Rome know I was cool, I walked into my dining room and looked down at Amber's lifeless body. Her eyes were staring right at me and she had a smirk on her face. It was crazy seeing her like that, and I wasn't going to lie, her death was always going to bother me. Her lying on the floor with a slit neck was an image that was going to always be embedded in my mind. I hated this was the way that we ended. I hated even more that I wasn't man enough to let her go when I should have, a long time ago.

Thinking back on the whole situation, I was selfish. I allowed her to play a part that was never meant for her, just because I didn't want to do my bid alone. All I was trying to do was fill the void of Aubrey and Kylie no longer being a part of my life. Seeing Aubrey with another man, no lie, it killed my spirit and knocked me off my high horse. I felt so dumb for fucking up what I had with Aubrey dealing with Cinnamon's street walking ass. I already had my STD testing done everything came back negative I swear she was next on my hit list if it didn't.

I was done with all of the games and bullshit. I wanted my family back. That saying, you never know what you have until you lose it was definitely true, because I missed the hell out of my little family. It was fucked up that I had to lose them twice to realize the lies and bullshit wasn't worth losing them. Lesson learned and I was fighting for my family. It might not have been tomorrow, but Aubrey would eventually give in. Plus, I knew for sure that she didn't want to be the cause of someone's death. Because next time, it was a bullet to the head, and no questions asked.

Chapter 6

Nasir

"Yo," I answered my phone without looking to see who was calling. I'd just bailed Quadir out and was currently waiting outside of the precinct for him.

"Nasir, are you ever going to talk to me?" Kari voice came through the phone. She was another problem that was currently on my hands. I couldn't believe I was stupid enough to knock her up again. She was barely in Amari's life, now she was trying to bring another child into this world only for her to not be there for.

"What do we have to talk about? Do you plan on having an abortion?" I queried, ready to hang up on her.

"We need to talk about everything. The baby, Rashawn and your little girlfriend, and why would you ask me do I plan on aborting my child?"

"Ava has nothing to do with our fuck up. I don't even know why you want to have another child. You barely a mother to the one you have now. Then you grimy as fuck for trying to blackmail Rashawn. I don't trust you. You already know he waiting to split your wig."

"You're going to let him kill me?" She cried through the phone. I couldn't even deal with this shit right now. It was just like Kari to get herself into some shit and then expect for somebody else to get her out.

"The question is why was you trying to blackmail Rashawn. What you need the money for." Waiting to hear the lie that came out of her mouth, I lit my blunt. Today was beyond stressful.

My brother got locked up on some bullshit charges. My beautiful niece was fighting for her life and Kai was probably having a nervous breakdown. I was stressed out and that wasn't even my drama.

"Nasir, you have to understand. My back was up against the wall. Back in Atlanta I was running with the wrong crowd of people and in the end I owed some really bad people a lot of money."

"What did you get yourself into?" My mind was now wondering. I knew it was weird as shit for Kari to just pop up in my life after three years. I was grateful because I now had my son, but hearing this new information, I knew she only came back to Philly because she was hiding out from some people. So this only confirmed to me that her interest was never being back in Amari's life. I could only be mad at myself because here she is now pregnant again and was barely a mother to our first son.

"It's over! I have nothing else to worry about now. The debt is paid in full. I know I put you in a messed up situation and I never really wanted to come between you and your family, but Rashawn was an easy mark. I know how he feels about Aubrey so I was planning on using that against him especially how careless and reckless he was being blatantly cheating on her. I was just doing any and everything to protect my son and me, but I'm not saying it was right because it wasn't." Hearing her say that she had to do any and everything to protect Amari had my full attention. The last thing I needed was for Amari to be dragged into Kari's bullshit.

"Kari, I'm telling you now, if your bullshit comes anywhere near my son I'm going to kill you myself." I heard her gasp.

"Nasir, how can you say that? I'm carrying your child, and like I said, I'll do anything to protect my son. I may not be the best mother in the world, but I would die before allowing anything to happen to my son."

"I hear you," I mumbled as I watched Quadir talk shit while

walking out the precinct.

"Can we talk about the baby I'm carrying? I truly want you to be a part of my pregnancy. You were cheated out of experiencing me pregnant and the whole process with Amari. I just want this time to be different. I really am trying to change for the better," Kari tried convincing me.

"Let me call you back," I responded then hung up before she could say anything else to me. To be honest, her question brought up a lot of thoughts that I've been trying to push to the back of my mind. One thing for sure, I didn't want to miss out on her pregnancy. Even though the first time around was completely her fault, I still didn't want to miss anything. However, I knew me wanting to be apart of Kari's pregnancy might cause a bigger strain on my relationship with Ava.

"Nigga," was all Quadir said as soon as he going the car. "Take me back to the hospital. I already know Kai stressing the fuck out."

"What the fuck happened?"

"Mikey's bitch ass got me arrested for assault, but that shit not going to stick because he edit the tape. All it shows on the video was me in beast mode fucking him up, but I have a tape, too, that shows his dumb ass pushing Kai, making her fall while she's pregnant."

"So how we handling him? I need to know because I'm not with the tit for tat shit." Mikey was always going to be a problem in their relationship. Even if it wasn't him, it was his delusional babymama. What she did was unforgivable and I truly believed jail was too nice of a punishment for her.

"Trinity is dead! As we speak, Majesty is locating her. I can't kill Mikey," Quadir explained, causing me to look at him like he was crazy.

"Listen, Kai's not built like that. If Mikey comes up missing or dead, she'll know it was me that made that shit happen. Regardless of all the fuck shit Mikey did, she would never be able to live happily knowing she was the reason for his death. Plus, death is too easy for a muthafucka like him. I would love to torture him. What I have in mind will torture him so bad that he'll want to kill himself." Quadir vented, looking like the tables were already turning in his head.

I didn't know what Quadir had up his sleeve but I knew whatever it was, Mikey was a done deal.

"So, wassup with the Kari shit. I can't believe ya dumb ass knocked that hoe up again." Quadir hissed. The way him and Rashawn were acting, you would've thought Kari said they were the ones that had gotten her pregnant. Yet, I understood their frustration. I'd fucked up big time and there was nothing I could do about it.

"Man, I can't even answer your fucking question. It wasn't like I was looking to get her ass pregnant, but shit happens. I wasn't careful. I know I slid up in her raw a couple of times," I admitted, shamefully.

"Are you sure she pregnant with ya fucking child? You know how that bitch get down."

My shoulder shrugged. "Man I guess."

"You fucking guess? Tell that hoe to abort that shit now! Nobody have time for her dumb ass games. She's barely a parent to Amari. Now you want to allow her to trap you with another baby that she barely wants. Kari have never had a motherly bone in her body."

Even though he was right, it pissed me off hearing the truth. It wasn't that I wanted her or anything like that because I definitely wanted my relationship with Ava to work, but at the end of the day, she was Amari's mother and the disrespect she received from my family was crazy. However, Kari played my ass like a fool last time, so they had all the right to dislike and question her motives.

"I don't want to have another baby by Kari. You know just like

I do that she's not having an abortion. So I don't have a choice but to step up and be a man about my shit. She says it's mine and I'm not going to walk away until I have proof the baby's not mine. Last time I believed what I saw and wasn't apart of Kari pregnancy with Amari. I wish I were around for that shit. Hell, I wished I were around for the first couple years of his life, but I wasn't because I didn't do things the right way and didn't get a DNA test," I stressed and that was the honest truth.

I could care less about Kari, but I would never leave her hanging again pregnant with my child, and I didn't care what anyone had to say about it. I didn't want to go against the grain with the whole situation with Rashawn. I knew Kari deserved the bullet, but yet and still, I couldn't allow Rashawn to take out the mother of my children, no matter how fucked up she was.

"Go to bat if you want for that bitch. You really acting like she didn't steal thousands of dollars' worth of jewelry from you. Nasir, I'm letting you know now, keep her away from the family and Ava. You've been really reaching with protecting her from Rashawn. Kari knew what type of nigga Rashawn was before she came up with her plan to extort money from him. You can't expect Rashawn not to handle her the way he sees fit."

"Rashawn need to worry about Amber's crazy ass!" I voiced, brushing off what Quadir said. Fuck it. What type of man would I have been to allow someone to come for my babymama? Quadir was pissing me off because if Kai were in some shit he would have been protecting her at all cost. Looking down at my phone that was now indicating I had a text, I saw it was a text message from Rashawn saying, *done.*

I guessed Amber was no longer a problem.

"Listen, all I'm saying is don't get to involve so soon. I'm telling you this because now if you get too invested and that baby's not yours, it's going to be a major hurt piece. Especially if you spending bread and preparing yourself mentally to have another child."

"I'll do what I see fit!" With that said, the rest of the ride to the hospital was silent. I appreciate the silence too.

I was taking everything Quadir said into consideration. Deep down, I knew Kari was notorious for passing another nigga's baby off on someone else. Prime example was Amari. She had Tony believing he was the father until he got a DNA test.

I needed to have a sit down with Kari as soon as possible. I planned on being there throughout her pregnancy every step of the way, but she needed to understand that there was going to be boundaries put in place. My relationship with Ava was something she would have to deal with and accept. Plus, I wasn't playing any games when it comes to her being a better mother. I would file for full custody for both kids and dictate when she would be able to see them.

Chapter 7

Aubrey

"**M**om! Daddy is taking us shopping!" An excited Kylie said, running into my bedroom without knocking.

Wiping my eyes that were filled with tears, I gave her a weak smile. "Oh yeah.... great," I then said, sounding everything but enthusiastic.

"What's wrong with you?" Kylie queried. I hated that she could sense that I was different. I was trying to deal with what happened to me that night, but it was hard.

"Nothing."

"You sure? Because I just told you daddy is taking us on a shopping spree. A shopping spree that we much deserves. Especially since he been a jerk these last couple months. I say we spend all his money and look pretty doing it." All I could do was laugh at this crazy girl. I felt bad for whoever son married her ass. At the age of nine she was telling me how to finesse her own damn father.

It had been a whole week since Amber held me hostage. Now I felt like I was in another hostage situation with my crazy ass ex. Rashawn had done moved all of his things back into my house. I wanted to protest so badly but I knew it would be a waste of time. I had been sneaking around texting Morgan. All I wanted to know was whether he was okay or not. When the street doctor came, he told us that Morgan's jaw was broken. The only response I received back was Morgan telling me that he was okay but to never contact him again. I was hurt because I truly liked him. Yet, I granted his wishes. The last thing I needed was for Rashawn to come through on his threat.

Getting in the shower, I allowed the water run all over my body. The shower had been my safe place. It was where I could let out all my frustrations in private. Rashawn had been watching me like a hawk, especially because of what I went through was so traumatizing. I could play tough all I wanted but that night with Amber, I knew was going to be my last. Amber wanted to kill me, and I had no doubt that she would have if Morgan didn't kill her first.

She was the worst kind of a dangerous person. I say that because she had nothing to lose. I just felt bottled up because I didn't want to tell anyone what happened to me. The way things were going, our family didn't need any more bad news. After shedding my daily tears, I washed my body, ready to spend family time with Rashawn and Kylie.

Pulling back the shower curtain, I let out a scream and almost fell in the shower. I was not expecting Rashawn's crazy ass to be sitting on the toilet waiting for me. I didn't even hear him walk in. I watched his eyes graze over my body, making me quickly grabbed my towel and wrapped it around me. It had been a while since Rashawn showed me any interest, and today was not the day I was going to bust it open for his cheating ass.

"What are you doing?" I questioned, stepping out the shower and finishing my morning hygiene. I could feel his eyes burning a hole in me.

"Aubrey, I'm not going anywhere! I want my family back. I'm willing to do any and everything to get us back to where we were. I know I haven't showed you these past couple of months, but I truly do love you. Yeah, I fell victim to the pussy that bitches was throwing at me, and I know it was wrong of me to run away from our problems instead of staying here and fix them." I looked at him like he was crazy. I had to stop him before he uttered some more lies that only he believed.

"That's the thing Rashawn, we didn't have any problems. We were prefect. We were walking down the aisle and everything. Amber was the issue! She been an issue since day one but we were moving on with our lives even with her craziness. You was the one that did a whole 360 after she shot up the wedding. You can try and put all the blame on Amber and how you thought you made her crazy when the truth is, having a family and being faithful was too much for you to handle. You wanted your freedom. You were lock up for seven years. Why would you want to be tied down to one bitch?" I looked at him and I could tell my words bothered him.

"Aubrey, shut ya dumb ass up, because everything you just said was bullshit! I was faithful and loyal to you since the day I met ya lying ass. Talking about ya fast ass was eighteen, all along you were sixteen. I'm not making excuses for what happened because I was truly on some fuck boy shit. Not only did I let you down, I let my daughter down too. All I'm asking is for you to allow me a chance to right my wrongs. I love you and I want you and Kylie back in my life." He leaned in and kissed the nape of my neck. It felt like he had the key and let the flood gates open. I swear my pussy was cussing me out because she knew I was about to reject his ass.

"Rashawn, let's get ready to go to the mall and spend family time. Kylie is probably waiting for us." I moved out of his way and headed to my bedroom and locked the door because I knew he would follow me. Pulling my underwear draw open, I saw my vibrator. As tempting as it looked, I needed to get dressed.

Fuck it! I thought as I pulled it out.

At this point in my life, I wasn't sure where I wanted things to go with Rashawn. I was happy with moving on, and Morgan was a lovely distraction from my failed relationship. However, now that Rashawn had basically put an end to that, I didn't want sex to have any influence on my decision making on where I wanted things to go in the future with Rashawn.

Laying on the bed, I unwrapped my towel and laid spread eagle. Turning on my vibrator, I placed it on my throbbing clit. I started imagining Rashawn caressing my body lovingly as he place sweet kisses along my thigh, leading up to my honey spot. I then imagined his tongue licking and sucking on my pearl as his hands caressed my breast.

"Rashawn," I moan as I felt myself ready to reach my peak. It wasn't long before I let go of a mind blowing orgasm.

"Damn baby," Rashawn's loud ass voice interrupted my fantasy. Jumping up, I damn near threw the vibrator across the room, trying to cover up my body. Rashawn was standing in front of my bedroom door with one hand in his pants stroking himself. "If you needed some dick all you had to do was say something."

"Get out!" I screamed. I was beyond embarrassed. Not only did he watch me masturbate, but he knew I was thinking about him while doing it.

"Alright, chill your horny ass out. Don't get mad at me because you being stingy with the pussy," he shouted over his shoulder.

"Aarrghhhh," I groan as he walked out of my bedroom.

After getting dressed, the ride to King Prussia Mall was filled with laughter from Kylie and Rashawn. He was seriously in the business of kissing some ass today. Before getting out of the car he'd already told us that we didn't have a limit. I swear I was going to have him regretting his words. I was definitely putting a dent in his pockets.

"I'm about to put some of this bags in the car," Rashawn suggested to me. We were now in the Gucci store and I was currently picking up some new heels and Kylie some sneakers.

"Okay," I mumbled. I couldn't lie, spending time like this together made me feel good, but I was still mad that he did me dirty. Like, he didn't even know how his treatment toward me was making me question myself as a woman. Every insecurity ran through my head. Cardi B said it best, Rashawn had me thinking I was flaw because of his inconsistence. And, what made it worse, the bitch he cheated on me with had nothing on me.

"Mommy, I want these," Kylie said, bringing me a pair of all white Gucci sneakers. They were cute and not too grown looking. Honestly, I was ready to go. We had spent about three hours in the mall buying a whole bunch of unnecessary things. Yet, I stayed true to my word, and me and Kylie put a dent in that black card Rashawn gave up so freely.

"Alright, I'm ready." I said as the sales lady came over and I gave her Kylie's sneaker size. "I'm getting these sandals and the pocket book to match." The sales lady smile before walking away.

"Mom, do you know her?" Kylie asked, pointing to some lady who was staring at me with the death stare. It was no other than the stripper that Rashawn was spending all of his time with. The same bitch who house I sent a U-Haul truck to, filled with his clothes.

"No," I answered and walked to the register when I saw the sale's lady come back with our items. I paid for our things then told Kylie to come on. I prayed I wasn't going to have to show my ass in front of Kylie today. I didn't want to, but I just knew something was about to pop off by the way she kept grilling me and my daughter.

"You sure? Because she keeps looking at us like she know us," Kylie said with much attitude. I could tell she was getting annoyed by the attention. Plus she knew it was rude when you stare at people, so I knew she was starting to feel uncomfortable.

"Just ignore people like that. Let's eat." We headed to the food court. I texted Rashawn to let him know where we were and he said he'll meet us there because he was going to Foot Locker to buy some sneakers.

"Excuse me." This bitch had the nerve to walk up to me and Kylie's table.

"You're excuse." I dismissed her. There was no reason why she thought it was okay to say a word to me, especially in front of my daughter.

"I think we need to talk. Where is our man? I've been calling him nonstop and he haven't been answering?"

"Bitch, our man, seriously?" This bitch couldn't have been serious. Obviously, she was delusional because Rashawn wasn't claiming anybody but me, and I didn't even want that. Nonetheless, this was what happens when a nigga let his side piece think she's more than what she actually is, a piece of ass.

"I didn't stutter." This stripper rolled her eyes with her hands on her hips.

"Sweetheart, he never been your man. Shit, I done packed all his shit and moved it to your house free of charge and ya dumb ass couldn't keep him there. Face it, you was nothing to him"

"Who are you?" Kylie asked with an attitude. I swear I hated she was so grown. I hated the fact that she thought she could jump in grown people conversation because right now wasn't the time. I knew this bitch was waiting to say some off the wall shit that would make me snap.

"Hey baby girl, you must be my new step daughter. I'm your daddy's girlfriend, Jasmine," she said then leaned over to give Kylie a hug. I lost my entire cool and stole this bitch in the back of her head, causing her to stumble away from Kylie.

"Mom!" I heard Kylie scream as Jasmine came full force charging at me, doing a windmill. I was so mad that I was entertaining this bullshit. We had everyone in the mall's food court full attention. I could see people pulling out their phones ready to put my black ass on World Star.

"Oh no." Kylie stuck her foot out, causing Jasmine to fall face first. The food court erupted in laughter. Picking up our bags I told Kylie to come on. We were just going to have to meet Rashawn at the car. I was done with the circus act.

"You little bitch!" Jasmine said, now standing up and had

pushed Kylie to the ground. Next thing I knew, all hell broke loose. Dropping my bags, I went straight momma bear mode on that hoe. She didn't even have a chance as I started to hit her with every combination. All I could see was red. Not only did this girl think it was okay to talk to me about Rashawn in front of our child, but to put her hands on Kylie was a huge no-no.

"Yo, what the fuck yall doing?" I heard Rashawn's voice before I felt myself being lifted off the ground.

"Put me the fuck down!" He did as I ordered and I snatched away from him. "Come on Kylie." I was so over Rashawn. Ever since he came back from jail and into my life it's been flipped upside down.

"Cinnamon, I know you didn't come from my babymama. That ass whopping your got from my sister wasn't enough to know not to fuck with me?" Rashawn hissed through gritted teeth.

"I know you not calling this bitch little pet names." Who the fuck is Cinnamon? Rashawn was about to get part two to this beat down.

"That's her name—well, her stripper name. I didn't care enough about this hoe to learn her real name," he expressed in frustration, like I was getting on his nerves.

"Rashawn," Jasmine begged for his attention. She could barely get herself off of the ground.

"Let's go!" He commanded, literally pulling me and Kylie through the food court and out of the mall.

"Rashawn, you need to handle that bitch! She put her hands on Kylie," I yelled as soon as we all got into the car.

"She did what? Why you just telling me now? You know that hoe about to go into hiding." Pulling out his phone, he told one of his runners to be park outside of her house. Then he made a second phone call to King Black, the owner of the KINGS strip club, to hit him up if she comes to work.

"Daddy, you were with that lady? That's why you stop being

around me and my mommy?" Kylie asked barely above a whisper. Looking back, I could see the tears in her eyes. She was really hurt from the way Rashawn treated us these last couple of months.

"Kylie, no woman could ever make me stay away from you. I will never leave you or your mom for anything or anyone. I was wrong and I needed to get myself together. I had some personal issues that I had to work out."

"Well, she said she was my step mommy. Is she the reason why mommy doesn't want to be with you?" She then asked and Rashawn turned to glanced at me with an apologetic look on his face.

"Me and your mom are together and will forever be. She can't leave me and I will never leave her, so don't worry about that lady. Daddy's going to take care of her," he assured Kylie.

"That's why we in this situation now. You taking care of bitches," I mumbled under my breath as we made our way home. I was so upset at the fact that once again Rashawn's drama had managed to affect me as well as my child.

Chapter 8

Mikey

"**M**ichael, you don't hear this baby crying?" My mom yelled, storming out of my kitchen and into the living room. I'd called her over here to take MJ with her, but instead, she stayed and started cleaning my house and expected me to take care of MJ.

"Yes, I hear him. I need you to take him and leave the house. I don't want him here!"

"What do you mean take him and go? This is your son Mikey! He didn't ask to be brought into this world. You need to man up. I'm so disappointed in you right now," she then voiced, picking MJ up and started to comfort him.

"I don't want him here! I'm about ready to drop him off at the fire station so they can put him into the system. I didn't ask for him to be here either," I mumbled, but by the way my mother's neck jerked, I knew she heard me loud and clear. Even so, what I said was the truth. I never wanted a baby by Trinity.

Thinking about Trinity had me seeing red. I truly wanted to kill her but nobody knew where she was. I'd called her parents multiple times, and when they finally answered they told me that they didn't know where she was. I couldn't believe she tried to kill Kai. Not only did she try to kill Kai, she sped up the divorce process. Yesterday, I received the DNA results in the mail along with our final court date. All I wanted to do was dwell in my own misery.

It was crazy that one forbidden night changed my life forever.

"Mikey..." My mom said, trying to hand him over to me. There was no connection between me and my son. Just the very sight of him disgusted me.

"No, mom! I'm telling you now, if you don't take him with you, he's becoming an orphan. Trinity knew what she was doing. I planned on signing over all my rights to her. She knew I didn't want MJ. That's probably why she tried to kill Kai. She think I don't want MJ because of her."

"Is that true? That's how you act? You was perfectly find with being in MJ's life and accepting him as long as he was a secret. Now Kai knows and wants a divorce you decided you're not going to be in your child's life." Only half of what my mother said was true. When MJ was secret, things were much better. I still had my life and my wife. Me not wanting to be in MJ's life had nothing to do with Kai. Kai would've never been okay with me not being in my son's life. It was just Trinity and MJ caused so much damage in my life and I wanted nothing to do with them.

"Are you excusing what Trinity has done to Kai?" I had to asked because she was coming off like running Kai over wasn't a big deal.

"God heavens no!" Mama Bullock gasped like she was appalled by my questions. "Trinity needs to be thrown in jail. I hope the police find her before those thugs Kai is mixed up with does. That's why you need to be here for MJ. He's going to lose one parent and he doesn't need to lose both. Remember, he's the innocent party in all of this craziness."

"He is. That's why I'm still willing to take care of him financially. Mom, either I sign my rights over to you or he will be a foster child. I'm not ready to be a father. To be honest he won't survive in my care. I'm telling you, taking him is in his best interest."

"Michael, I'm so disappointed in you. I truly don't know who this person is sitting in front of me. The son I know would never turn his back on his child. A baby he prayed about and finally received."

"I didn't pray for that little nigga! I pray for a baby with my wife. I'm done speaking to you about this, I'm not being a father to that baby. He was a mistake! His mother trapped me. Point blank and period. She knew what she was doing. Just because her delusional ass went off the deep end to try and kill Kai, is not going to make me change my mind. She should of taken him on the run with her dumb ass." I stood up and started packing MJ's diaper bag. I needed them out of my space. This was going to be the last day I would set eyes on my son.

The sad truth about it, I felt relieved.

"Just give me his bag, Mikey!" My mom screamed and I obeyed her command. Grabbing MJ's car seat, I opened my front door to head to her car. It was déjà vu from when I threw Trinity out my house.

"I hope you know you going to regret ever turning your back on this child. You and his mother are pieces of shit." I knew she was mad if she was belittling me. But, oh well. I said what I said and I meant it, too.

Watching my mom put MJ in her car, I saw my cousin Cream pulling up. Me and Cream use to be best friends when we we're little. He was my best man in my wedding. Our relationship fell off because Cream was starting to get heavy into the streets, and I wasn't with it. Not saying I was better than him or anything, I just wasn't dumb enough to put my life on the line for some fast money.

"What is he doing here?" My mom asked, looking Cream up and down. My mom didn't get along with anyone from my dad's side of the family.

"Nice to see you too Aunt Mary." Cream chuckle. "I see ya mom still an evil bitch," he said loud enough for her to hear.

"Arrrghhh," my mom screamed before hopping in her car and pulling off. She hated Cream since he was little. She always said he was the most ignorant child she's ever known.

"Why you have to say that?" I shook my head. The feelings my mother had for Cream was mutual. Cream always felt like my mother was judgmental and my father was a bitch to allow her to drive a wedge between him and his family. My father hadn't spoken to his siblings in years, and the last time everybody saw each other was at my wedding.

"What the fuck you want?" Cream asked with a menacing look. I was starting to wonder if he heard about all of the drama that I had going on.

"Damn, why you looking at me like that. I can't just want to chill with my cousin?"

"Nigga, we haven't chill since ya fucking wedding day. I know you want something wassup."

Cream was always straight to the point, and wasn't with no bullshit. Looking around, I tried to find the words to say to him. What I was about to ask him may seemed outlandish but desperate times called for desperate measure. Quadir was now out of jail and I know he was looking for me. When he was release he gave the court the video from the shop showing that he was protecting Kai.

Of course him throwing the first punch was edited out but when the judge saw me pushing a pregnant Kai to the ground, the case was thrown out.

"I need you to take care of a problem for me. I'll pay you whatever you want, but I need you to kill someone or at least point me into the direction of a hitman. Shits real and I needs to dead this nigga before he do me." Cream looked at me and busted out laughing like I'd just said the funniest shit ever.

"Nigga I know all the trouble you're in and you fucked up." Cream then shook his head walking towards my bar pouring him a shot of Tequila. "I thought you didn't associate with people like me. Now you looking for me to help you."

"I'm coming to you because I know you'll be able to get the job done. Plus, I know whoever you hook me up with is going to be discrete."

"Why are you doing this? I know it's because of Kai. You did shorty dirty, now she fucking with someone else. Take your lost and move the fuck on!" Cream said, now getting ready to leave. I already knew he was going to be mad. One thing he hated was to be used. I hadn't spoken to my cousin in a minute and the first time I do I asked him to orchestrate a hit. Yeah, I probably would've reacted the same way.

Even so, I inquired, "Are you going to help me or not?" I wasn't trying to hear the bullshit he was spitting. No one seemed to understand where I was coming from. Everybody thought I'm just this delusional husband. But what everyone failed to realize was, I'd loved Kai since I was in grade school. Love like that didn't go away. I broke our vowels on a drunken night, but so did Kai.

We we're supposed to had stayed together for better or worse, and now that we were at our worse, she didn't want to have anything to do with me.

"Nigga, you don't get it do you?" Cream shook his head. "Quadir is the fucking hit man! I can tell you now your days are numbered. All I can advise you to do is enjoy your last days with your son because you're not going to have many."

"Wait!" I panic. "What you mean he's the fucking hitman? Can you find me someone to take care of him? Don't you have connects with the Black brothers."

"Who do you think he work for." Cream said, walking out my front door. Like he didn't even tell me that my life was on borrowed time. I had to get to Kai and apologize. If anyone could save me from her lunatic boyfriend it was her. "Oh yeah, and stay away from Kai." With that said, I watched my cousin jump in his car and pull off. Walking back into my house, I slammed the door. Everything was messed up, and I should've of left well enough alone before things got this far.

Chapter 9

Kai

"**M**ommy, loves you Miracle," I whispered into her ear than gave her a soft kiss as she laid perfectly in Quadir's arms. I loved watching him with her. He was so gentle and so protective of her.

"What about daddy?" Quadir queried, looking me up and down and causing me to blush. I swear it was going to be a long six weeks. Ever since we made love for the first time, Quadir couldn't keep his hands off me. Now with the baby weight going straight to my ass, my breast was huge and stomach basically nonexistent due to all of the breast feeding and pumping, Quadir acted like this wait was slowly killing him. Trust, I give him head damn near everyday, probably twice a day, but I was feening for my sugar walls.

"You know I love you, babe." I leaned over, placing my full lips on his, kissing him with so much passion that it set my soul on fire.

Those little three words *'I Love You'* held so much weight and I meant them so much. Quadir brought so much light and positive energy into my life, especially when I needed it the most. He taught me how to love again. After finding out about Mikey and his infidelities, I was broken. Broken beyond repair. Quadir taught me to move through the hurt and pain, and to love my self again. My self esteem plummet through the floor.

In the beginning, I blamed myself for the demise of my marriage. That was until Quadir helped me understand that Mikey's decisions and actions had nothing to do with me not able to have children. I loved this man for helping me build back up my confidence and love me through all of the craziness.

"See, that's how yall got Miracle now," Ava said, causing us to break our kiss.

"I don't mind giving her another baby. Plus, I think Miracle needs a little brother or sister so she won't be lonely. I like my women barefoot and pregnant," Quadir said, rubbing my stomach. Swatting his hand away, I looked at him like he was crazy. I wasn't planning on getting pregnant anytime soon. My pregnancy with Miracle was a hard one, and I wanted to enjoy being a mother to her before I had another child—Which I could barely do, being that I needed help myself.

After the accident, I was left with a broken ankle and a torn Achilles tendon, thanks to Trinity. Plus, I get back to the flow of things with work and school. I haven't told anyone yet, but I applied to go to college to finish getting my degree. I stopped going to school when I helped Mikey pursue his dreams of owning his own fitness gym.

"Don't look at me like that. Shit, the way your holding out it's a guarantee that you going to get pregnant as soon as I slide up in you."

"Yall nasty," Ava said, turning her face up like something stank.

"Quadir, give me my grandbaby," my mom voiced, surprising me. I didn't see her come in with Ava. I was so appreciative of Quadir family and mine. Everyday, someone was visiting Miracle in the NIC-Unit. Either it was our parents, my sisters, or Nasir and Rashawn. My support system was everything and I was truly blessed to have them.

"Mom, I'm holding her today. I swear yall be hogging her. My niecey pooh a week old and I still haven't held her," Ava pouted like a baby.

"Did yall wash your hands?" Quadir asked, pulling out his hand sanitizer, waiting for them to hold their hands out. It was ridiculous how over protective he was over Miracle.

"Boy, yes! I washed my hands." Dana hissed, "You act like I didn't raise three kids my damn self. And, one of them you keep trying to stick your little pecker in." All I could do was laugh.

"Whatever, this my baby and Ava you can't hold her, you look sick. Your eyes red and puffy. Better luck next time."

"Shut up, fool! I have allergies." Ava rolled her eyes and went to sit in the chair next to Miracle's incubator.

"Babe, stop!" I laugh because Ava was out her looking crazy. She always have bad allergies, ever since she was a little girl.

"I'm about to head out. I have a couple appointments at the shop," Quadir announced, handing Miracle to my mother then gave me a kiss. "I love you."

"I love you too, babe."

"Bye mom and big head." He gave my mom a hug then mushed Ava in the back of her head before quickly walking out the door.

"I love seeing you in love, baby." My mom smiled at me.

"Mommy, he makes me so happy. I never thought I would love anyone except Mikey, but Quadir came into my life and opened my eyes to real love." I then looked down at my baby, as my smile grew wider. "I still can't believe I'm a mom. Right now, I just want everything to be about me and my family, and I can't wait until this divorce is over."

"It will be soon," Ava said rubbing my back in comfort.

"You're right, it will be because I'm going to Mikey's house right now to make him sign these papers. I'm so over him and his crazy ass babymama. I want him out of my life forever."

"Kai..."

"No, mom," I said cutting her off. "I'm over this. All of it has gotten way out of hand. Not only was he lying to prolong the divorce, but his babymama tried to kill me, then on top of that, he had the bright idea to have Quadir locked up for assault the same day I gave birth to my daughter. Ava, can your drive me there, and mom can you stay here with Miracle. If not, I'll just let the nurses know I'll be back and catch an Uber to his house. Either way, I'm making him sign the divorce papers."

"Kai, I'll take you. The last thing your cripple ass need to be doing is demanding someone to do something when you can barely walk." Ava shook her head while handing me my crutches.

"Just hurry back because I'm not lying to that man of yours," Dana said before placing her attention on Miracle.

"You won't, thank you," I said, grabbing my crutches and made my way out of the NIC- Unit, with Ava following closely behind me. I already had the papers in my purse. Today, I was truly on a mission. I'd been waiting for the perfect time to go to my old house to have a one on one with Mikey. I just never could get away from Quadir. He'd been waiting on me hand and foot and I wasn't about to let him know my plan. If I did I was pretty sure Mikey would end up in a body bag. I didn't want Quadir to go any where near Mikey. Knowing Quadir temper he would be going to jail for murder. Mikey pulled the ultimate low and got Quadir arrested. So I just wanted this chapter in my life to be over.

"You ready?" Ava asked, pulling up to my old house. There were so many memories, love and happiness. But then there were also the dark memories of multiple miscarriages, lost love and drama of my husband's babymama making her presence known by throwing their child in my face.

"I been ready!" I voiced, getting out of the car. I turned around when I heard Ava's door close, and saw Aubrey, "Where you going? Why are you here?"

"I'm going in there with your cripple ass! You act like Mikey is in his right mind frame. That nigga would kidnap your short and hold you in the basement somewhere, and tell me how I can explain that to Quadir. Bitch you crazy!"

"And, did you think yall bitches was going to pull up on this nigga without me?" Aubrey said walking up looking like she was ready to fight. She had on an all-black PINK sweat suit from Victoria Secrets and some black Timberlands with a scarf on her head.

"I'm not even here for the bullshit. I'm just here for him to sign the papers."

"Okay and we're here to make sure he sign those bitches." Aubrey was already hyped up already. Making my way to my front door, it swung open before I could knock.

"Kai!" Mikey shouted, pulling me in for a hug. I was hit with he most horrid smell that could've came from a grown ass man. Pulling away, I got a good look at Mikey and he looked horrible. He was gaining weight in the worst way. Looked like he'd put on a good thirty pounds. I didn't notice the weight gain before, but I definitely saw it now. He no longer had the body of a fitness coach, and his clothes were too small and dirty. His hair was nappy and matted. I knew he couldn't tell me when the last time he went to the barbershop let alone took a damn shower.

"Mikey, can we come in?" I asked.

"Yes, baby, this is your house. You will always be welcomed here. How are you? I wanted to visit you in the hospital but you know you got this little restraining order against me," he ranted all in one breath, sounding like a sad puppy.

"Mikey, do you know your baby mother was the one who hit me and tried to kill me and my baby."

"I know, that's why when I see her I'm going to kill her myself. She knows how much you mean to me. She's just mad because I don't want anything to do with her or my son. Never did I think she would go that far and try to kill you. Baby, you have to understand I would have did everything in my power to stop her if I did know."

"So yall just going to ignore this fucking stench? Like what the fuck? When the last time your dirty ass washed up? Shit, look at this house. All these take out container and old food laying around. Mikey, you need to get yourself together. I know you don't have your child around this shit," Aubrey ignorant ass had to say.

"I hope not because I would straight up call child protective services on your neglectful ass." Ava co-signed, turning her nose up.

"Why are they here?" Mikey asked, visibly irritated by their presence.

"Yes, tell him why we're here so we can get the fuck up outta here. Is that a fucking roach? Oh, hell naw, speed this shit up. I ain't trying to take any critters home with me." Aubrey said, picking up her purse from the sofa and checking it.

"Kai, can we talk in private please?" I just shook my head no. "Listen, I'm begging you to come back home. I made one huge mistake that I will forever regret in my life, and I will do everything in my power to make things right. We're not perfect and we we're supposed to fight through any downfalls that may have came our way."

"Nigga, nobody wants to hear you begging and pleading," Ava said in a bitter tone. It was crazy how at one time they truly loved Mikey like a brother, but now they couldn't even stand him. I guess that's what happens when you caused this magnitude of pain.

"This is what I'm talking about." Mikey roared, pointing at Ava and Aubrey. "You have people in your ear telling you what you should be doing. Look at your sister, neither of them been married yet they're here encouraging you to throw ten plus years away like I didn't mean anything to you. Look at how Jaxson dogged Ava's ass, yet she gave him chances after chances."

"Mikey, really? I didn't hide a whole child from my spouse. You were married and fucked a bitch the same time your wife was suffering from a miscarriage. Fuck you!" Ava was heated.

"Naw, fuck you ditzy hoes! Aubrey, you have the nerve to be judgmental when she hid her baby from her babydad for years, all because she found out *she* was the side chick. Kai, you can't be seriously listening to these people." Mikey was on one today calling out everybody flaws but refused to see his.

"Michael! I'm here for you to sign these divorce papers!" I pulled out the divorced papers and a pen. The look on Mikey's face had me speechless. It was like I was watching his heartbreak, literally, in front of me. I almost felt bad, but I had to remind myself that we were at this point in our marriage because of him.

"Naw, I'm not signing shit!" Mikey shook his head. "Kai, I'm fighting for you till the end."

"No, what you going to do is sign these fucking papers, Mikey!" I yelled. I was fed up with his delusional ass thinking that this marriage still had a chance. "Look at all you and your retarded ass babymama put me through. Just sign the papers and I can promise that Quadir won't hurt you."

"Bitch, don't make promises you can't keep! You know just like I do that his time is limited. He got that man arrested," Ava said, looking at me like I was stupid.

"Naw, Quadir knows I would never want someone's blood on my hands, and he loves me enough to respect my wishes. Now Trinity? I can't save that hoe. Sign the papers Mikey!"

"No," he answered. I was over everything. Standing up, I swung my crutches right at his head. Ava and Aubrey jump right in swinging on him.

"You crazy bitches. Get the fuck off me," Mikey yelled and pushed me, causing me to fall back being as though I only had one good leg for true support.

"Ahh, fuck no!" Ava screamed and pulled out her taser and started tasing him as Aubrey started kicking him all over his body.

"Ahhhhhhh! Shit......Stop!" Mikey begged as his body shook

from the volts of electricity going through his body.

"Who you think you fucking with Mikey?" Ava taunted tasing him some more. Honestly, I thought Ava and Aubrey were getting a kick out of beating Mikey up. Pulling myself onto the couch, I watched in amazement as my sisters went ham on him

"Mikey, I'll tell them to stop if you sign these papers," I said. With all the strength he had in him he muttered the words, no, while shaking his head.

"Ava, turn that shit up to the highest volt," Aubrey instructed Ava. Doing as she was told, Ava sent another bolt of electricity through his body. I swear the neighbors could hear Mikey screams, but Ava wasn't stopping.

"Ahhhhh! Please...... I'll sign." He could barely get out his words because of the pain he was in.

"I bet your dumb ass will," I mumbled. Ava and Aubrey back up off of him and gave him some room to get himself together. After about five minutes. Mikey pulled himself off the floor. Standing up, I saw a wet spot running along the front and side of his grey sweat pants.

"Damn, Ava, you made this nigga pee himself." Aubrey said as they busted out laughing. I hated I had to embarrass him like this, but he kept wanting to make this difficult. Sitting on the couch, I handed him the pen and papers.

"Kai...."

"Mikey, there's nothing you can say or do that will change my mind. I want to move forward with my life, with my daughter and man. Now do us all a favor and sign the papers." I cut him off. Mikey reluctantly sign the papers, and the smile that spread across my face could be seen a mile away. I couldn't wait to give these to my lawyers. A bitch was finally divorce.

"Please go," he said just above a whisper. However, I heard him clear as day, and he didn't have to tell me twice. Standing up, I took one last look at my ex husband. The love of my life since I was in grade school. The man who taught me everything about love and everything about heart break. The man who had my heart and loyalty and lost it. In hind sight I was grateful for his mess up because without it I wouldn't have my Miracle or her daddy.

"Bitchhhhhhh," Aubrey said, as she looked at Ava and me. All we could do was bust out laughing.

"We fucked him up!" Ava shook her head thinking back on our actions. Mikey was jacked up. I know Ava cause some damage tasing him. Aubrey had probably cracked some of his ribs the way she was kicking him, and he had a huge knot on his head from where the crutches hit him.

"Well, it worked. I'm a free woman now."

"Ayyyyyyyeeeeeee!" We laugh as we all started twerking until my phone started to ring.

"We need to throw you a divorce party," Aubrey said heading to her car. I could see the wheels turning in her head. I didn't even care because this was a time for celebration, and I couldn't wait to show Quadir I was finally all his.

Chapter 10

Kari

"I'm outside," Nasir said as soon as I answer my phone.

"Are you com..." was all I could get out before I heard the phone click in my ear.

Today was my first doctor's visit. Nasir have been really distant, and this was actually the first time I would be in his presence since the whole barbershop fiasco. I was hitting four months of pregnancy and I was already over it. Especially since the fact I never planned on having this baby. Plus, I was pretty sure it wasn't Nasir's with the way I was busting it open and throwing this ass in a circle to stack the paper I needed to pay Snake off.

Walking out my front door, I saw Nasir sitting in his black on black Range Rover, talking on the phone.

"Babe, I'm going to call you back. I love you too." Whatever the bitch he had on the other line had his dumb ass smiling like he Cheshire cat. "Ava, stop playing, you better be at my house with my little niggas. Plus, Amari been asking for them to spend the night."

All I could do was roll my eyes after hearing that name. Go figure. He was talking to that ghetto fake ass bougie bitch. I swear I never seen Nasir so far up someone ass, and it was ridiculous. I just couldn't wait until Snake's grimy ass snatched her up. She would be out of Nasir and Amari's lives for good. Even though I didn't plan on staying around, I would never want Nasir and Ava to ride off into the sunset together and raise my son in some happy bullshit blended family. It might've sounded selfish, but oh well.

"Hello," I finally spoke after he complete ignored the fact that I was in the car. We've been driving for the last ten minutes and his ass was just bobbing his head to the J. Cole new album K.O.D.

"Wassup?" He kept it short.

"I guess you can't talk to me. Is your bitch that insecure that she has you on a leash?" I snapped. His nonchalant attitude was driving me up a wall. I hated that fact that he allowed Ava to dictate what we had going on.

"Kari, chill with that name calling shit. Ava could care less about the fuck up situation that we have. Stop blaming my treatment on you on everybody else except yourself. You the one that have me on the outs with my cousin because ya dumb ass was trying to extort money from him. That nigga want to kill you and only holding out because you are pregnant with my child." He glanced over in my direction. I could see he was very frustrated. I wanted to feel bad but at the end of the day, I was doing what I had to do to keep Amari safe.

"Nasir, how many times I have to tell you I'm sorry. I told you the whole truth. I was only doing that for our son, and sorry, I would do it again if it ensure Amari is safe," I said in a matter fact tone.

"If Amari was in so much trouble why didn't your dumb ass come to me about the money instead of trying to set up Rashawn and stealing my jewelry with your thieving and crack headed ass mother. I know her scheming ass was down for the lick."

My breath got caught in my mouth when he accused me of stealing his jewelry. He hit everything on the head. I never wanted to steal from him that day. It was all Kyra. All I wanted was money. I was going to play dumb because I wasn't admitting a damn thing.

"Amari was in trouble and lets be realistic, you weren't going to give me the money to pay my debt. And I didn't steal shit from you! So stop accusing me of that bullshit. You the one handing your keys out to every bitch that bust it open for you."

"Bitch, the only person who have a key to my house is Ava. The only reason you had one was because of Amari, to bring him to my house when I was closing the shops late. Now I know ya retarded ass stole my shit because you're wearing the fucking diamond tennis bracelet that I bought Ava." I looked down at my wrist and curse myself. How stupid could I be to wear something that I stole from him in front of him? "Yeah, shut ya dumb ass up!"

I didn't even respond to his disrespectful ass. I just allowed us to drive the rest of the ride in silent. All I knew was that I wasn't taking this beauty off my wrist. Fuck that! That hoe Ava walking around with a diamond ring on her finger. Anyone would believe they were engaged as to how big that ring was, and they talking about it being a promise ring. Walking in the doctor office, you wouldn't think we weren't together because his immature ass sat across the waiting room caking up on his phone.

"Kari Clinton," the nurse called my name, alerting Nasir and me that it was time for us to be seen. I watched him stand up and I actually took in his appearance, and damn how did I fuck my relationship up with him. This nigga was dress in a black Burberry polo shirt, some black jeans and matching Black timberlands boots. His dreads were freshly retwist and braided back.

Nasir looked like a damn snack.

"You can follow me back. You must be dad?" The nurse asked Nasir.

"That have yet to be proven. I'll claim the baby once the DNA comes back. Other than that, I'm just here to make sure she is doing what she need to do to make sure the baby come into this world healthy. You know, just in case it's mine." Embarrassed was an understatement. I couldn't believe he even let that shit come out his mouth. Granted, it was true that he was probably the last candidate in 'who's your baby daddy' mess I'd created, but he didn't have to put me out there like I was some hoe.

"Okay," The white nurse turned bet red. "I need you to give me a urine sample than Dr. Howard will be right in."

When she walked out and closed the door behind her, I spoke up, "Really, Nasir? That's really a fuck up thing to say." I was beyond piss and I truly felt that he needed to apologize.

"Kari, go to the bathroom to take your piss than change into this hospital gown. What's fucked up is that your bum ass out wearing shit you stole from me. You lucky your pregnant if you weren't I would definitely have Ronnie come beat your ass," he said, referring to Rashawn gay ass sister who looked like a whole linebacker.

Huffing and puffing, I made my way to the bathroom and to handle business. I was so over this damn doctor visit already. All I wanted to do was go home. Maybe ask if Amari could come over. I haven't seen him since the barbershop and I truly felt like the worst mom in the world. But I knew I needed to let Nasir calm down after I'd drop that pregnancy bomb on him. Walking back into the room I saw Dr. Howard was already inside smiling all up in Nasir's face. The bitch acted like he wasn't here with his babymama. I swear I hated female doctors, especially with the one who don't know how to act. The way she was flirting with Nasir was unprofessional and I was ten seconds away from snapping out.

"Ummm hmmm," I cleared my throat, rolling my eyes at Nasir who wasn't paying me any mind.

"Hello, Kari, it's nice to see you. The last time I saw you was when we did the first ultrasound to see how far along you were," she said with a smile that looked genuine. Not realizing she just let the cat out the bag.

"Why the fuck haven't you been coming to the doctor regularly?" I knew that would catch his attention. Truth was, I didn't plan on keeping this baby so I didn't give a fuck about the baby's health. It was just going to get chopped up when I got the abortion.

"Because, Nasir, I didn't know if I wanted to continue to do this on my own. I know your with Ava and I didn't want you thinking I was trying to trap you."

"But you are trapping me with this baby! To be honest, I don't want another child by you. You're a fucked up individual and mother." Those words broke my heart. I knew I wasn't a saint nor was I going to win the mother of the year award, but to hear him say it with so much disgust in his voice only proved to me that no one would ever love me. I wanted to be a better mother, but life had a way of bringing the worst out of me. It was time for me to grow up and as soon as Ava was out of the picture, I was taking Amari and my new baby and move away from Philly.

They say if you want to feel unconditional love to have kids, because they loved you no matter what. Nonetheless, I felt Amari was still young enough for me to change my ways.

"Listen, Nasir, the door is right there. You don't have to stay, and I can care less if you're in this child's life. You've been disrespecting me since I sat in your car and I'm over the fuckery," I said, and the room remained quite as Dr. Howard preform her routine task. She did want to take another ultrasound just to see how the baby was growing, especially for the simple fact that my last time here was a couple months ago.

"Kari, you need to take better care of yourself for the baby sake. The baby is underweight for how far along you are, and dad do you mind stepping out I have to speak to mom about something private." Dr. Howard asked Nasir who completely ignored her. He didn't trust me so he wanted to be here for everything.

"He's not going to leave so just say what you need to say. Plus, you've already been unprofessional smiling and flirting with him. There's no reason to stop now," I said with much attitude laced in my voice.

"Fine, your pee came back positive for marijuana. Also, you have a very bad yeast infection that should have been taken care of. Vaginal infections are very serious. If it goes untreated it can cause a miscarriage. I shouldn't even have to explain what the harm of smoking and drinking can cause a fetus. If you want a healthy baby, you need to get your act together. If this continues I can guarantee that you will not be leaving the hospital with your baby. Child protective services will be called," Dr. Howard said what she said and left out the office, but not before telling me to set up my next appointment and she was writing me a prescription for antibiotics. Nasir got up and walked out of the office. I knew he wanted to act a fool, but this wasn't the right place.

When I was done making my next appointment, I was almost afraid to walk out to the truck where he was.

"Kari, wassup with you smoking while pregnant? You want our baby to come out with some type of birth defect or something like that? You want to spend months in the NIC-Unit after you deliver because you neglected the child you decided to bring into this world? Or worst, you want the state to take your baby away from you?" Nasir threw questions after questions at me with much concern dripping from his voice. I was surprised. I just knew we were about to have a full blown shouting match.

"Nasir, my life have been so fucked up since the day I listen to my mom and cheated on you with Tony." I finally admitted not only to him but to myself too. If I could turn the hands of time around I would. Nasir was the only person who showed me genuine love and I messed that up listening to my mother and thinking about money, instead of being the supportive girlfriend when he decided to pursue his dream head on. Now look at him he owned a chain of barbershop across the city of Philadelphia. "I'm done with the games and bullshit. I just want to be a better mother to my kids."

"I hear you, and I want that too, but I'm a firm believer of actions because baby girl everything you just said to me you said it before. Kari, our situation is not ideal, but I have you. So, do your part and be a good mother."

The rest of the ride we had small talk about getting me a better apartment or maybe a townhouse for the kids and me. He even gave me the okay to call him wen ever I needed him for the baby or Amari only, but I took what he gave me at the moment. I was truly looking forward into turning over a new leaf, even though I planned on disappearing after this baby. The goal was just to have my kids with me.

"Make sure you get your prescription from the CVS in the morning," Nasir reminded me as he pulled up to my house.

"I will." I smile and hopped out the car. This pregnancy was kicking my butt, but I was just happy Nasir and me now had an understanding on our situation. Walking into my apartment I smelled Snake signature Cuban cigar. "Mom what are you doing!" I scream, quickly shutting my door. The scene in front of me was something no child should witness their mother doing. She was sucking my landlord's dick while getting fucked from the back by the maintenance man. I could tell she was high out her mind. I'd recently gotten my apartment back after doing some odd favors myself. I had some money from some of the johns that I'd stolen money from on top of them paying me for any sexual act I preformed.

"Don't mind her candy girl, your momma still paying off your debt." Snake said, blowing smoke out his mouth while walking from the kitchen.

"I thought my debt was set. I gave you all of Ava's information." I looked at him like he was crazy.

"I know, but Ava's not in my possession right now. You know I have to rile her in slowly, but in the mean time you and your mama still on the clock."

"But I'm pregnant." I whispered.

"And you owe me a quarter million dollars. Manny specially requested you. He loves some pregnant pussy. Strip and get my money." Snake ordered, looking like the devil himself. Walking towards Manny, he licked his lips in anticipation for all of the sexual favors I was about to do with him. Pulling his dick out of my mother's pussy, he pulled the condom off and started stroking his little dick to make it hard again.

"What can I do for you daddy," I moan, playing my part. Deep down, I felt like dying a slow death.

"I'm trying to see what that mouth do," Manny responded, and I drop to my knees taking him whole, giving him the best head he'd ever had in his life.

Chapter 11

Sharonda

I received a call from my boss telling me to report to Human Resources immediately. She never told me why and only said it was mandatory. I found that weird, especially since I was currently on my two-week vacation.

I had no clue what it could be about, but I was thinking positive. I had recently put in for the position of the Chief of Nurse. So maybe I had received the job. Walking into the corporate office, I notice news crew lining up around in front of the hospital. As I made my way inside of the corporate building I felt like all eyes were on me. I smile and spoke but I barely got a response back. All everybody did was glance and started whispering to the person next to them. Taking a deep breath, I walked into the conference room.

Everyone in the room face was emotionless as they all looked at me. Looking around everyone that was someone was in the room. I was starting to believe this was not about a promotion. I've been promoted before and it never gained the attention of my hospital president, Dr. Ashby and my boss. They all had looks of disappointment covering their faces.

"Ms. Jacobson, please sit." The President demanded in a deep stern voice instead of asking. I looked at my boss Barbara and her white skin was a red as the devil. She looked like she was ready to blow a gasket.

"What's this about?" I tried to whisper, now knowing for a fact that this had nothing to do with the promotion. All Barbara did was put her hand up to silence me. I wanted to slap it away and out of my face. Barbara would've never dared to do that shit if she wasn't in a room full of our peers.

"I'll let you see what this is all about, but before I do I have some simple questions for you. You were trained and learned about all of the rules and regulations we uphold as a hospital. You were trained on patient services and ethics. You do know right from wrong, Ms. Jacobson, correct?" The President asked, looking directly at me, waiting on my response.

"Yes sir," I answered.

The lights dimmed and the projector was turn on. What I saw on the screen brought tears to my eyes instantly. How could Trinity do this to me? I don't care how much we got into it I never took it as far as to ruin her livelihood. The farthest I went was tagging Mikey on that Facebook post because she broke up my relationship with Kasim. I couldn't understand for the life of me why I held on to my friendship with Trinity for so long. I guess it was because she was my friend when no one wanted to be. But throughout the years all she did was sabotage every relationship I had. She hated when men found me attractive or me succeeding in life in my career. Trinity was a person who never wanted great things to happen to her friends if nothing was happening to her.

I looked around the room and saw my superiors were watching the video of me drugging Kai again, to place her back into her coma. I was beyond embarrassed by my action and watching the video made me feel even guiltier. Kai looked so terrified I couldn't believe I use to laugh and joke about this with Trinity. This was disgusting and I could tell my peers felt the same way by the looks on their face. Thinking back I didn't know why I would even jeopardize my job like this. Yeah I had a little grudge against Kai for slapping me at the baby shower, but losing my career was not worth the shits and giggles. I had to be a sick person to harm her while she was so defenseless.

"There's no question asked, you are fired! I know you notice the news crews lining up alongside of the hospital. Within the next couple of hours your face will be plastered all over every news station and new outlet. Not only did your bad decisions make you lose your job but your tarnish the reputation of the hospital, and possibly brought on a possible lawsuit from the patient." The president barked. My bad decision caused me everything, and I would never be able to work in the healthcare system again.

"I'm truly and deeply sorry. I'm embarrassed by my actions. No matter what, I should have never allowed my personal relationship with the patient to allow me to bring harm to her. I took an oath and I didn't uphold that oath. I brought Mrs. Bullock unnecessary harm." I held my head up high and apologized. I knew my apology was nothing compared to the damage I just caused, but I deeply meant every word I'd just spoken.

"How many times have you done this?" Dr. Ashby asked.

"It was only that one time. I was getting blackmail to do it again."

"I guess the person who was blackmailing you is the one who sent the video and pictures of the texts."

"Yes," I muttered lowering my head.

"I defended you when her boyfriend said you shouldn't be her nurse. Do you know if anything would have happen to Mrs. Bullock or her child relating to the obsessive amount of medicine you gave her, everything would have fallen onto my lap? My career would have been at stake too. I'm just happy I followed my gut feeling and remove you off of the patient care."

Dr. Ashby was right, not only we're my actions stupid, they were also selfish. I didn't think about anyone but myself. I put everyone career at risk who was sitting at this conference table just to be petty. I couldn't believe Trinity's hateful ass took things this far, and to see this was the length she would go when she didn't get her way was beyond hurtful because I was truly a good friend. Now I could see why I was her only friend.

"All I can advise you is to get a lawyer because you're definitely going to need one. It Now I may start my press conference. Please leave your badge on the table and anything that is in your locker will be mailed to your address. You are no longer allowed at this facility unless it's for medical attention. If you are here for any other reason, you will be arrested for trespassing," The President said before standing and walking out the door to do some damage control.

I got up holding back the tears that was threatening to fall. Placing my badge on the table, I quickly and quietly walked out of that room. Walking through the human resource office, I literally felt everyone judgmental eyes burning a hole through my body. I never felt so vulnerable in my life. I had truly just ruined my life and now I knew I should've never told Trinity anything about what I had done.

I wanted to say I couldn't believe she would do this to me, but then I could. Trinity always had been a vindictive little bitch. She ruined my life and I was going to do the same to hers I knew she was currently at her parents' house. That was her M.O. Every time she got herself into some trouble she would run to her mommy and daddy for help and protection. I knew for a fact that Trinity caused that hit and run at the courthouse. I put two and two together when I saw on the news that Kai was the victim and I remembered her car was damn near totaled. Pulling out of the parking lot, I turned an hour ride trip into thirty minutes to Trinity parent's house. Shaking my head, I hopped out of the car and walked up to the Hughes house. I could never understand how a person coming from a God loving family could turn out to be so evil.

I run the doorbell and waited patiently for someone to answer. Mrs. Hughes opened the door with a shocked expression then gave me a genuine smile.

"Hey Sharonda what brings you by here," she asked loud enough for everyone in the house to hear. Her actions alone let me know Trinity's hoe ass was in there probably hiding. I pushed my way into their house without invitation. I was going to beat

Trinity's ass! I was planning on giving her the ass whooping she deserved a long time ago.

"Trinity!" I screamed, making my presence known.

"Sharonda, she's not here. You need to leave! Barging into my house like you lost your damn mind." Ms. Hughes lied through her crusty ass chapped lips. I ignored her and made my way up the steps to Trinity old bedroom.

Kicking opened her door, I found Trinity trying to put on some sneakers. She knew I was here to let my hands do the talking. I tackled her like I was on the Eagles football team. Yes, I was a big girl and I used my weight to my advantage, and trust me I went straight beast mode on her skinny ass. Grabbing Trinity by the hair with my left hand, I started throwing haymakers with the right. Trinity was landing some punches but the way my adrenalin was pumping, I didn't feel anything.

"Sharonda, I'm sorry," I heard Trinity yell out. Hearing her trying to apologize only made me madder. Kicking her in the stomach, I watched my powerful blow send her flying back onto her bed. I charge to her as she rolled off and landed on the floor and started stomping her everywhere on her body.

"Stop it, both of you!" Mr. Hughes snapped, pulling me off his conniving ass daughter who was currently crying. "What is the matter with the both of you? You are best friends," he demanded to know.

"That bitch ain't shit to me!" I was fuming, trying to pull away from his tight grip. At this point, all I wanted was for him to let me go.

"Sharonda, I could have you arrested for assault and trespassing," Mrs. Hughes said in a condescending tone, helping Trinity off the floor.

"Go ahead, so I don't have to. You know it's a cash reward out for anyone who can give the police a tip on the hit and run at the courthouse. Who involve Mikey's wife Kai. Trust and believe, I'm going to cash in, since this bitch just took away my livelihood and my career." I roared and watched as all three of their mouths dropped open.

"Just calm down Sharonda, we can get through this. Why did you come here and attack Trinity?" Mrs. Hughes inquired. Now she was singing a different tune.

"Because your whore of a daughter ruined my life." Trinity put her head down in shame. I would think she was actually sorry but I knew better.

"What did you do now girl?" Her father demanded to know.

"I sent some videos to her job and to the news stations. She was giving Kai unauthorized medicine to keep her in a coma."

"Tell them the whole truth! You were blackmailing me to keep doing that to Mikey's wife, so your delusional ass can have your fake ass family. Mikey never wanted you. Trinity, you were a mistake and took it upon yourself to have a baby by a man you only knew for a of couple hours. You sit here and blame everybody for your failures instead of realizing you are the reason for them. When will you get that through ya head?" I shouted.

"Is this true?" Mr. Hughes asked for confirmation.

"Yes," she said just above a whisper. Her father looked at her and shook his head. Probably trying to figure out where he went wrong in raising her dumb ass.

"Why the hell would you do that?" Mrs. Hughes asked but she was looking directly at me with a look of disgust plastered all over her face.

"Excuse me?" I know she wasn't going to skip over the part of her daughter blackmailing. The fuckery in this family was crazy.

"You heard me. Why would you allow somebody to blackmail you? And from what Trinity told me is that you did this yourself. At your own free will, because Kai slapped the shit out of you at the baby shower. You know Trinity is sick in the mind. Why wouldn't you think she would use that against you? You cause your life to fall apart, so don't blame anyone else but yourself."

"That bitch ain't sick! She just a delusional hoe and it doesn't make excuses for the fuck shit she does. I'm going to leave now. Trinity you ruined my life, so I'm going to do you one better and make sure it's not long before you sit in a jail cell."

I could finally see why Trinity was they way she was, her parents never held her accountable for her actions. Like, seriously? What type of white shit they're on. '*She sick.*' Really? She sounded like the media when some white kids shoot up the school or churches. The shooter was always mentally ill, let them claim it. They never looked at it for what it truly was. Like the shooter of Charleston, Dylan Ruff. They wanted people to believe that he had mental issues instead of it as a racial planned massacre. Trinity's mom fitted right into the bullshit, mental illness was not an excuse. Plus, nothing is wrong with Trinity. It seemed like the only time they would hold Trinity accountable for anything was if her actions were embarrassing them and their name. Like she did at the baby shower.

Walking out the front door, I slammed it shut. I was so into my emotions that I never noticed the black Tahoe truck sitting across the street with all tints.

"Yo' ma," some sexy ass nigga called out to me. I wanted to keep walking but with the way my day was going I needed some positive attention.

"Yes?"

"Come here," he waved me over. Putting a little pep in my step and switch in my steps, I walked over to the truck like I was on America Next Top Model. I was so focused on the sight in front of me that I was taken by surprise when I saw a figure walk around the car in all black. Stopping in my tracks, I felt my body began to tremble as I came face to face with the last person I wanted to be with.

"You thought you was going to get away with the bullshit you were pulling?" Quadir asked with a sadistic smile. All I could wonder was how he knew, but then I remembered, more than likely my face was plastered all over the news.

I could feel my phone vibrating over and over again in my purse, but I ignored it.

"No… Wait, let me explain." I screamed before the Tahoe door open and I was snatched inside. All I could do was start praying to my Lord and savior, asking for forgiveness, because I knew my life was now over for real.

Chapter 12

Trinity

Sharonda popping up at my parent's house caught me by surprise, and seeing how easy it was for her to find me had me no longer feeling safe here. I'd been staying with them since the day of the accident. I begged and pleaded for them to help me. My mother stepped right in and helped. She even took my car to the junkyard so it could be stripped for scraps. My father was against me coming here. He still hadn't forgiven me about the whole Mikey's situation. So, he definitely didn't want to help me after I told them the truth about running Kai over with my car. Yet, somehow, my mother persuaded him to let me stay.

I missed MJ so much and was now regretting my choice on leaving him with Mikey's family. Who knew how he was being treated. I secretly prayed that my baby was staying with his grandparents because I knew for sure that Mikey wouldn't take care of him. Looking back on my actions, I was so stupid. I begged my mother to get MJ, but she was convinced if she did everybody would know where I was. That was mainly, because my parents didn't have a grandparent relationship with MJ.

"I have to go," I mumbled as my father paced back and forth looking like he was trying to wrap his brain around something.

"I agree," he finally spoke. Stopping his movement, he looked me straight in my eyes. My father had been against me being here since the day I came begging for help.

"No, we have to figure something out. Do you really think that Sharonda is going to call the cops on you? Seriously, you and Sharonda have been fighting since yall was little," my mother asked, causing me and my father to look at her to see if she was serious for asking me that dumb ass question.

"Yes, I just single handedly ruined her career! Sharonda and me had plenty of arguments and we even came to blows before. I even went as far as to steal her boyfriends, but I never went this far to destroy her livelihood. I made this girl lose her job." I mean, I knew how hard Sharonda worked to become a nurse. I remembered her long nights studying and working during her whole college career just to survive. She wasn't born with a silver spoon in her mouth like me. She came from a family where she was the first to graduate high school let alone attending and graduating college.

"We don't have to figure anything out! Trinity got herself in this mess now she has to get herself out. I'm not going to jail for harboring a fugitive. They have an award out for her arrest," my father barked with so much bass in his voice. I knew he meant business.

"Seriously, John? Our daughter needs our help, and you're ready to turn your back on her."

"Listen, we've been saving Trinity since she was old enough to walk. I swear she's a demon child! I noticed her conniving ways back when she was in the first grade and did little things to get people in trouble when she didn't get her way. Let's not forget the time she lied on Sharif and said he raped her when in all actuality, she became obsess with the idea of them being together after she suck his little dick in the school bathroom. I swear she's the result of God punishing me for my sins many years ago," he fussed, digging in his pocket and grabbing a knot of money.

Probably the money from last Sunday's collection.

I hated my father. He always wanted to pass judgement but he's the main one robbing his member's blind. The members thought that the money they were putting in for collection was going to help the church and its up keep, but in all reality, all the money from the church he used for his personal needs, like the gambling problem he thought no one knew about. I watched with hate in my eyes as my father grabbed my old high school book bag and started packing the little bit of clothes I had there.

"John, please," my mother whispered, harshly, with her eyes damn near popped out her head.

"Damn, it seems like everybody's secret is coming out today," a deep voice boomed through my bedroom. I was so tuned in to what my parents were hiding that I hadn't notice the two figures standing by my bedroom door.

"Majesty... what are you doing here," my father stuttered. I could see the fear etched all over his face. I was wondering the same thing.

"Yeah, how did you get in my house? We paid our monthly debt." My mother demanded to know, as she placed her handed on her hips. My father snapped his neck so fast in her direction that I thought it made a complete circle. I knew she messed up by the way my father was now looking at her.

"Watch your mouth! This doesn't concern you." Majesty said in a way that caused the hairs on the back of my neck to stand straight up. "Your girlfriend let us in on her way out."

"You." Quadir pointed at me. "Get up and let's go!" Hearing his voice had all of the blood draining my body. Sharonda used to tell me how he would curse people out in the hospital over Kai. Like, he was so overprotective that he made sure only certain people could care for her while she was in the coma. So I was pretty sure this wasn't a social visit.

"She's not going anywhere!" my mother yelled, standing in front of me. She had always been my protector. Quadir let out an evil chuckle.

POW!

Quadir pulled his gun out and shot my mother right in the head without blinking twice.

"Noooooo!" I let out a gut-wrenching scream as my mother's

body fell back on me. I could feel her blood soaking through my shirt as I laid her on my bed.

"Daddy, do something!" I yelled but the look on his face let me know my mother death would never be avenged. The look plastered on his face wasn't even one grief or anger, it was more of a look of acceptance and acceptance.

"Trinity its nothing for me to do. She's dead and you're probably next. Please go with these gentlemen," he stated calmly like he wasn't handing me over to my killers on a silver plate.

"Daddy, please help." My eyes were pleading for him to do everything in his power to save me. For Jesus sake I was his daughter. How could he not fight the men who'd killed his wife and was trying to kidnap his daughter?

"Trinity, with you gone from my life everything would be so much better. You and your mother have been a burden in my life for so long that I'm actually relieve that I will never have to worry about yall again."

"I'm your daughter."

"But you're not!" He said shocking the hell out of me. How could he deny me when all he ever had been was my father?

"You and your mother are just alike, weak over flesh. Weak over men and borderline retarded when a man or the devil shows yall hoe ass some attention."

Shocked and hurt was an understatement.

John Hughes never claimed me as anything but his daughter, and I'd never known my mother and father to have any marital problems. They always seem to be the perfect couple. Hearing him now had me feeling as if my whole life was a lie. When I was little my father was always strict and harder on me than my mother. I always got what I wanted because my mother could make my father submit to her at the snap of her fingers.

"Trinity, I resented you ever since the day you were born. You're the product of your mother jezebel ways. I'd been sterile all of my life. So when she came to me saying she was expecting our first child I wanted to divorce her, but I'd just became the pastor. How would the congregation look at me knowing I was divorcing my wife? So I stayed and tried to be a good father and husband. But you are just as conniving as you mother. Do you know she was giving my hard-earned money to your father? My best friend and they were living a separate lie on my money. You remember your uncle Kenny, right?"

Tears started to fall from my eyes. I knew my father was about to reveal the truth of Uncle Kenny's untimely death. I remember Uncle Kenny very well. Not only was he my father best friend, him and my mother had a very close relationship. He even treated me like a daughter. When he died my mother was so broken up when they found his body in the dumpster around the corner of the church with a bullet in his head.

"Your uncle Kenny's death wasn't just another unsolved murder in the city of Philadelphia. It was a professional hit made by this man. I paid him to kill your mother, too, but I decided against it being as though I would have to be the one left to raise you. Seeing that he's in my house uninvited, I guess they're here for you, because I made my monthly payment for my personal debt that is owe to the Black family."

"Daddy, please help me!" I cried, trying to grab him only for him to brush me off like I was a piece a lint on his shirt.

"He can't help you!" Quadir finally answered the question for my father.

"But, he can! I promise you. He has so much money. Please, if you just allow him to help me." I begged Quadir hoping to see a little bit of leniency. Money made the world go round and everybody needed it.

"Bitch, my girl and daughter's life is worth more than money. You know you fucked up! I need my payment in blood, especially since yall dumb bitches don't know how to leave well enough alone." With that being said I felt the impact of his gun smashing into my head. Then everything started to fade black.

Waking up, I was laying on my back. Looking around, it looked like I was in an abandon warehouse. Trying to move my arms and legs, I realized I was strapped down like I was a prisoner on death row getting ready for the lethal injection. I swear I felt like I was in a Jason horror movie, especially with all of the different types weapons that align the wall. I tried praying to god but I knew even he couldn't get me to escape this death I was anticipating. All I could pray for was my death to be quick and fast.

Thinking back, I hated that I allowed myself to go semi—delusional over Mikey.

I missed my son and now I would never see him again. His last memory of me would be me placing him on the steps and running off. I knew he was just a baby now, but I truly believed that The Bullock's would tarnish my name and reputation as a mother when my son started to ask questions. I hated I tried to kill Kai; because now I realized her being out the picture didn't change Mikey in any, shape, way or form. Mikey just didn't want us in his life. My failure to believe the obvious just allowed my son to become a parentless child, my mother to be murdered, and Sharonda to lose her job.

"I see you decided to join us," Quadir voiced like I had a choice and he didn't just knock me out. He gave me a warm smile like we were long lost friends see each other after years apart.

"Please, let me go," Sharonda's voice rang out as she sobbed. I could tell she was scared too, and it broke my heart that I'd drag her into my mess. Even though Sharonda drugged Kai on her own, I didn't have to blackmail her or send those videos to her job and the news station. Nobody would have known what she'd done if it wasn't for me.

"Naw," Quadir responded then took the remote to the chair I was laying in and sat me up. With the chair holding me in a vertical position, I was able to see Sharonda hanging by the rope that was tied around her hands on a pole. Quadir even had her feet tied and she was dressed in nothing but her bra and panties. What made it worse was the fact she was dying in holey grandma panties and a too small bra.

"You see this shit?" Majesty spoke out, turning through the channels on an old TV that was sitting on a crate. Every news channel he turned to was covering the huge malpractice suit the hospital that Sharonda was working could face. They actually had the video playing. For some odd reason looking at the fear Kai had displayed over her face was really messing with me.

"I'm pregnant. I'm sorry for everything I did but Kai and your daughter was fine after I did that. I wasn't the one who tried to kill her," Sharonda rambled throwing me under the bus. Her throwing me under the bus was no use for the simple fact that I knew neither one of us was walking away from this alive.

"Please, just let her go. I'm the reason for everything," I begged. I didn't want another child to hurt because of me. I figured I'd shoot my shot and try one good deed before I die, maybe God will open those pearly white gates for me. Quadir and Majesty both remain silent but gave me a look that told me to shut the fuck up.

"Let's get this shit over with! These bitches blowing my high with all this begging and pleading," Quadir mumbled as Majesty got up from his chair. They both were dress head to toe in some protective jump suits. One of those protective suits that a person would wear it they were in close contact with someone with the Ebola virus or dealing with hazarded chemicals. Quadir grab the end of the rope that was tied to Sharonda hands and pulled it so she was lifted higher into the air. She was hanging above one of those sinks that connected to the washer machine to drain the water.

"Put the stopper in and pour that acid into the sink." Quadir commanded. Sharonda was screaming and shaking so much that I thought he was going to drop her big ass, but he was strong as shit holding all that weight up.

Tears fell from my eyes as I watched and heard her praying a begging God to get her out of this situation.

"Do you think I care about your fucking baby? Did you care about mine when you decided to give my girl extra medicine to stay in the coma? Making her miss half of her pregnancy. Then this dumb bitch pressed over some dick and calls herself trying to kill my girl," Quadir snapped.

"I'm so sorry." was all Sharonda could get out before he started lowering her body into the acid. With her feet going in first, she let out piercing screams so loud a death man could've heard her. Quadir slowly loosened the rope, causing more of her body to go into the sink. After she was waist deep, he pulled her out the acid. Most of the skin on her legs was gone and the upper half of her body was currently melting away. It looked so gruesome that I couldn't imagine the pain she was going through. She had even past out from all of the screaming and pain.

I couldn't believe I was actually seeing her leg bone.

Majesty grabbed a chain and locked it around her mutilated ankles and feet. Once he had her secured, he instructed Quadir to untie her hands, and now she was hanging upside down by her feet. The looks and Quadir and Majesty were one of pure bliss as they casually talked and joked around while I watched them torture my best friend to death.

Turning on the water in the double sink, Quadir allowed it to fill up as Majesty now lowered Sharonda's body head first into the sank. After making sure was secure on the pole they left her hanging as the water continued to fill up in the sink. I could hear Sharonda faintly crying, than hold her breath as the water surpassed her head. Thirty seconds later I saw her body seizing and I could tell that she was drowning. No matter what Sharonda did, she didn't deserve to die that slow death.

"She a goner. How you want to dispose her body?" Majesty queried.

"Place her body in the acid. I only want her to be identified by her dentals." Quadir answered and then looked at me. I knew I was next. I just didn't want my death to be that awful, but I knew it was going to be far worse, being as though I'd tried to kill Kai and the baby she was carrying.

"Ready to meet your maker?" Quadir asked me, like he was asking me a regular question or some shit. Picking up a syringe, he filled it with something. I couldn't see the name on the bottle, but I know it wasn't good. "This is Ketamine, also known as Special K. It's a drug that makes you *paralyzed* in a sense. You will be alert and able to feel everything that I will inflict on you, but you will not be able to talk or move."

Instantly, the tears started to pour as I felt him inject me with the drug. I knew what I was about to endure was something for the history book in torture. I should have taken heed to my warning when he beat up Mikey's ass, not once but twice. Majesty walked up to him with a blowtorch. Quadir looked at the blowtorch like it was a new toy. Turning it on the highest it would allow, he placed the flame on my legs. I felt my skin melting and burning off. I wanted to scream. I wanted to move. But I couldn't do either.

Even if he didn't give me the drug, I was strapped down like I was a prisoner. He tortured me by placing the blowtorch on each one of my limb and torso. I now knew why Sharonda passed out. The pain was unbearable, and I found myself passing out as well.

When I'd finally came to, there was a floor length mirror standing in front of me. Somehow, Quadir put the contraption around my head and in my mouth. It was all metal and it seemed have been a mouth clamp because both of my cheeks was spread wide apart, so all thirty-two pearly white was on display. Quadir was holding a pair of plyers and started to pull my teeth out one by one, and it wasn't long before I passed out, again. The last time I came to I saw Majesty and Quadir smoking a blunt.

"Looks like little mama up again." Majesty smirk with his sadistic smile, looking like the joker himself.

"I see. Flip the switch! I'm done torturing bitches for the night," Quadir said and Majesty walked to the side and flipped the switch that was on the wall. As soon as he turned on the switch, I watched through the mirror at my own death. The clamp that was hooked into my mouth was pulling farther and father apart. It wasn't long as I felt my jaw breaking and the skin on my face being torn apart. I prayed through the pain that death was near and that my son forgave me. Before I knew it, I felt my soul leaving my body only to lead me to the fiery gates of hell.

Chapter 13

Ava

After watching Kai boss up on Mikey, it had me reevaluating my situation with my own man. I was so ready to be done with Nasir, because I wasn't trying to deal with Kari and her nonsense. But then I had to ask myself, why would I give Kari what she wanted. Nasir genuinely made me happy and I felt stupid that I was ready to give up on my happiness over some jealous ex. Plus, as many chances that I gave Jaxson broke ass, I was willing to make things work through the drastic changes that was occurring in his life. Don't get it wrong, I wasn't settling for any bullshit either. If Nasir wanted this relationship to work he had to come correct.

Tonight was our date night and I was on my way to drop the boys off to their father. Jaxson was currently living with his new girlfriend, the hoe Nevaeh that he had all up in my damn house when I was on vacation with Nasir. After the whole baseball bat situation Jaxson fell back, and this was the first time he was spending time with the boys. His excuse was that he'd just started a new job and was doing major overtime to stack up his money. I didn't care for his excuses because I wasn't the one he was disappointing.

Jaxson had to explain himself to his kids, not me.

"Yall ready to see yall daddy?" I asked Noel and Noah.

"Yeah, we miss him so much," Noel smiled. I was happy that they were excited to see Jaxson. Jaxson have been a good father. It just seemed like every time we go through something he just distanced himself from the kids. Pulling up in front of the apartment building. I popped the trunk to pull out the boy's sleeping bags and book bag with their clothes inside.

"Ava!" I heard Justice voice yell from across the street. I was surprise to see her here because Sharell always had a problem with Justice being over my house until we squashed our beef. I guess she was really off her bullshit. Ever since that dinner we had together with her boyfriend we'd been cool and cordial, and even met up a couple of times to get the kids together.

"Hey, baby girl. Wassup Sharell?" I smiled as Justice walked over to my car and started unbuckling her brothers from their car seats.

"Hey boo. You met this girl he's living with now?" Sharell asked, rolling her eyes. She hadn't been feeling Jaxson since he showed his entire ass at the damn restaurant, embarrassing himself.

"Girl, yes, and I tell you, it wasn't a good one. I literally kick this bitch out of my house." I chuckled, thinking back to that night.

"Wait! I know his disrespectful ass didn't have that girl up in your crib," Sharell said in shock, but I didn't really know why because that nigga was fucking her while living with me and driving my car. However, today wasn't the day to bring up old memories, especially since we were trying to better our relationship for the kids.

"Daddy!" Noel, Noah and Justice scream causing me to look up. All I saw was them running full speed into their father's arms. The smile on his face showed me that he'd missed his kids just as much as they'd missed him.

"Hey yall. I have somebody I want yall to me," Jaxson said as his girlfriend walked up behind him. She honestly looked nervous as she snuck glances at Sharell and me. We were looking at Jaxson who still had yet to acknowledge us. "This is my girlfriend, Nevaeh."

"So, this her apartment?" Justice asked and I tried not to snicker.

"Yes, but we live her together," Neveah answered.

"Dad, is you ever going to have your own place? Or you just going to live with every girlfriend you have?" Me and Sharell's mouths dropped open from Justice's question. Jaxson looked like a deer caught in head lights and I could tell the wheels in Neveah's head was turning, probably thinking was he only with her for a place to live. All I could do was pray for the girl because dealing with Jaxson, she was going to need all of the prayers she can get.

"Justice, watch your mouth!" Sharell corrected her daughter. "Nigga, you don't see your baby mamas over here?" I cringe at the word babymama, because to me, the word babymama had such a negative cognation. I felt like baby mamas were women who are bitter an upset that they were no longer with the father of the child.

"I'm not his babymama, I'm his children's mother." I let her know, looking at her like she disrespected me in the up most way.

"Bishhhhhh, same difference with your fake bougie ass." All I could do was shake my head because Sharell just didn't give a fuck about how ignorant she just sounded.

"Wassup yall? Thanks for bringing them over. I didn't think yall would."

Sharell was the first to respond back. "I know, that's why I brought Justice ass right over here."

"Why wouldn't we? You're their father. Just because shit happened doesn't excuse your from your responsibility."

"Ava, I know. I'm just surprised, especially after everything that went down." Jaxson admitted. "Ava, I want to apologize about that situation too. That shit was fuck up and foul. Even though I was mad I shouldn't have never disrespected you in that way period," Jaxson said, and I just shook my head. "And Rell, I'm sorry for showing out at your little dinner with your friend. I just want all of us to be cool and be able to co-parent on some real mature grown people shit."

"Nigga, we been on that type time. You're the one in your feeling because we were hopping on some new dick." Sharell shot back, not even caring that our kids were listening. I swear this girl had made some progress, but damn, she had some ways to go.

"On that note, yall ready to go inside?" Jaxson turn to the kids than looked over a Nevaeh.

"Hey, Ava, can I talk to you really quick?" Nevaeh asked. Looking down at my watch I seen it was almost six o'clock and I was supposed to meet Nasir at the movies at six thirty, but I guess giving her a couple of minutes of my time wouldn't hurt.

"Hey, I'm Sharell. What you need to talk to her about?" Sharell's nosey ass said, standing right beside me waiting for Neveah to start talking.

"Its nice to meet you, but I rather talk to her in private. What I have to say to her doesn't really concern you." Nevaeh sneered. I could already tell that they weren't going to get along.

"Naw, boo, whatever you call yourself about to do, dead that shit if you're not going to come correct, because I'm not with the bullshit." Sharell warned, looking Nevaeh up and down like she was shit on the bottom of her shoes. Rell was on one today but what got me was that this bitch was really riding. You would've never guessed we couldn't stand the sight of each other once upon at time.

"Nevaeh, you might as well say what you need to because she's not going anywhere," I stated the obvious, ready to leave.

"I just wanted to apologize for that little situation that happened at your house a couple of weeks ago. Yes, Jaxson lied to me and I was dumb enough to believe the bullshit, especially with all of the evidence around me." I guess she was referring to the pictures that I had all over my house of the boys, my family and me.

"Yet, you have him living in your house." Sharell chuckle, making Nevaeh feel dumber than she actually looked. I could tell with the look on Nevaeh's face things was about to turn left.

"Sharell, you're a changed person, remember." I tried to remind her to keep her pettiness at bay. "Nevaeh, its cool. I'm over that. I'm just happy the nigga is out my house. So, *thank you*," I smiled while she shook her head before walking towards my car with Sharell hot on my heels.

"Girl, you should have snuffed her ugly ass. They're mad disrespectful." Sharell always wanted some drama to pop off.

"Rell, I'm too old to be fighting. That shit is for the birds. Plus, my kids are staying at her house. I will not create unnecessary drama and have her treat my kids like shit. The way I see it, she did you and me a huge favor by taking Jaxson's ass off our hands. We have a much needed break from the kids. Shit I'm happy with this 'me time' I'm about to receive."

"Now that you said it like that, I am too. I convinced Jaxson to keep Justice for a week and Ian is taking me to Miami. Damn, I hope my pettiness don't make her send Justice home early."

"Girl, you know Jaxson not going to let that happen," I assured her.

"Yeah, you're right." Sharell then looked around. Jaxson and Nevaeh were already in her apartment building. "Let me stop being mean to her because all of us played dumb behind Jaxson. I was the main bitch turned side bitch, and you just let that nigga use you," she said causing me to snap my neck in her direction. "Relax bitch, we have grown and move on to bigger and better things."

"Sharell, bye," I laughed while shaking my head. "Fucking with you, I'm going to be late for my date."

"I'm just saying, we been there and done that. Hey, what size do the boys wear? I want to bring them something back from my trip." I ramble off their size. "Alright are yall still coming to Justice's dance recital?"

"Yes, we will be there."

"I should have the tickets when I come back from my trip."

"Okay, just call me," I said right before hopping in my car and pulling off. I wanted to go to the Movie Tavern. I love that movie theatre because you could sit down and eat and drink. Picking up my phone I called Nasir but my call went straight to voicemail. I wanted to let him know I was running a little late. Pulling up to the movie theatre, I didn't see Nasir car. So, I decided to just get the tickets and wait for him. All of my calls were going to voicemail and I was trying not to get worried. He didn't call me and tell me that something had come up, and we missed the movie for the 6:30pm showing. So, I grabbed some tickets for the 7:30pm one. As times went on and on, and still no call from Nasir, I started to get pissed.

Not only was he standing me up, but also, I had wasted my damn money on these movies tickets. Looking down at my phone and the time, it was now 7:15pm. I was over it. I tried to call one last time and of course I got the same response, which was hearing his damn voicemail.

"Fuck it," I mumbled as I watched a teenage boy and his mother walk up to the movies. I could overhear him telling his mom that it was his treat. "Hey, what movie are yall going to see?" I asked.

"We were going to see the Avengers. Was it as good as everybody say it is?" The boy replied.

"I'm not sure. I didn't see it yet. I have two tickets for the 7:30pm show, though." I handed the tickets out to them as I smiled. "Take these because I'm not using them."

"Are you serious? We can't take your tickets," His mother said, declining my offer.

"Yes yall can! If yall don't take them, they're going in the trash. Plus, I love what I'm seeing. I just hope when my son get his age they take me out to the movies or something fun. It's a Saturday night and instead of him spending it with his friends or girlfriend, he's actually taking the time out to spend with his mother, and I find that dope." I smiled, placing the tickets in his hand.

"Thank you," The boy said, smiling, before him and his mother walked away.

"It looks like I'm not the only one that got stood up tonight." Some random man said walking out of the movie theatre and towards me.

"Excuse me?" I snapped, getting a better look at the guy. I realized he was the man standing behind me in the ticket line.

"Hi, I'm Semaj. I noticed you give your tickets away. So I figured that the person who was meeting didn't show. My date didn't show either."

"Okay," I chortled, giving him an annoyed look. Did he really think it was a great way to start a conversation? I was already in my feelings and wasn't sure if I should be piss or worried that Nasir stood me up. It wasn't like him to not communicate with me.

"I didn't mean to offend you." Semaj ran his hand down his beard. "I'm just saying, we both came here to see the movie and I saw you give your tickets away. I'm not really trying to waste my money, so do you want to watch the movie together?"

"Ummm. I don't think that's a good idea, but thank you anyway," I nicely rejected his offer.

"No strings attached, ma. Shit, you don't even have to sit next to me. All I'm saying is, why waste the night away being mad. You came here to enjoy yourself and you should do that. I'm not bad company if that's what you're worried about. I swear I ain't." He displayed a smile, showing off his pearly whites. His little game was working. I did want to see the movie and I knew had I'd gone home I would've been sitting there all alone. Nasir obviously wasn't worried about me. So, why not see this movie with this stranger.

"Alright.... I'm Ava by the way."

Chapter 14

Semaj

I'd been following Ava for quite some time now, and being up close and personal with her, I could see why Kari was jealous of her. Her beauty was breathtaking and there was no denying that she would make me big money. Too bad I'd met her under these circumstances because if I'd met her before the craziness with Kari, she definitely would've been my wife, or at least my bottom bitch.

If you hadn't figured out who I was by now, I was Snake, and my name rang true to my character. I was the grimiest nigga you could ever meet. I was a pimp, a human trafficker, and taker. I was the best stick up kid that'd stepped out of the state of Georgia. My motto was to get money any way necessary. I didn't have a conscience, so, no I didn't feel bad for what I planned on doing.

Ava was just a casualty in this sick game I was playing with Kari. Kari was a mistake that should have never happened. I fell for a bitch with a big booty and a nice smile. I had her ass living the life, and I really thought she would be the Bonnie to my Clyde. I had the A on lock when it came to pimping and robbing niggas. The only muthafuckas I didn't mess with was those Black Brothers and anyone affiliated with them. Pharaoh, King and Majesty reign supreme through all of the states in the United States. I even tried to get down with them but my reputation proceeded me. They straight up told me that I was snake and couldn't get down with the way I moved. Rejection was a bitch but I would never go against them. That was death sentence that I wasn't applying for.

I had crazy money falling in my lap and I was cool. I trained Kari to run my business while I did my little bid. I gave the bitch everything that she wanted and needed. I knew my niggas thought I was crazy leaving mostly everything I had to her but at the time she seem like the only person I could trust. The niggas in my crew were just like me, crab in a barrel and just waiting for an opportunity for someone to mess up so we could come up, but imagine my surprise when Kari robbed me for this bum ass nigga, Dice.

I was the laughing stock of my crew.

I knew Kari would never be able to pay me back. My initial plan was to come back and kill her. However, when I seen that she was living carefree in Philly. I decided to fuck her whole life up, starting with pimping her and her mother out. When Kari's mother came up with the idea to kidnapping her son, my plans changed all together. Her babydad was making some nice money with his chain of barbershops he had around Philly. I was definitely planning on getting some of my money back. I didn't care if the muthafucka had to sale a couple of his business, I wanted my money.

"I want to thank you for giving me one of your tickets," Ava smiled as we made our way out of the movie theatre. Watching the movie with Ava was cool and I could tell she was a down to earth person. Tonight wasn't the night I was going to snatch her up. I had to get her to find an interest in me and when she had a guard down that's when I was making my move.

"Your welcome. I couldn't let a pretty girl as yourself go home mad. You made my night by keeping me company."

"Aww... Well, whoever stood you up doesn't know what she just miss. Thanks again. Hopefully, I see you around again," she said, and even though she was just being polite, I had to shoot my shot.

"We can make that a guarantee if you put your number in my phone," I suggested.

"Naw, she's good my nigga!" Some oversized bearly ass muthafucka said, stepping in between us. Looking at him, I knew exactly who he was. He was Kari's baby father. I couldn't wait to get my hands on his money.

This nigga walking around looking like money! I thought to myself, looking at his watch and chains, down to his shoes.

"Thanks again, Semaj. You have a good night," Ava deescalated that situation with the quickness.

"No problem, beautiful. I'll see you around," I smirked and walked off to my car. There was no doubt in my mind that I would be seeing Miss Ava really soon. My mind was on my money and that's what Ava was, *my money*.

Chapter 15

Nasir

I was fucking up big time, and I had nobody else to blame but my damn self. Juggling being a parent, my relationship with Ava and being there for Kari was starting to become too much. Here I was, looking at Ava and about ready to smack the shit out of her for being up in another nigga's face. I didn't know what she called herself doing, but she was about to have a nigga go to jail.

"You care to explain yourself?" I barked, causing a few people to look in our direction.

"No the fuck I don't, asshole! You're the one who needs to be explaining your fucking whereabouts, or did you forget that your dumb ass is three our late for our date?" Ava snapped, looking me dead in the eyes. I couldn't lie, she had me stuck like a muthafucka. "You know what? Goodnight, Nasir." She shook her head, hopped in her car and drove out of the parking lot.

Fuck! I muttered, walking back to my car. I didn't even know why I came at her like that, knowing my ass was dead ass wrong. The only reason why I knew she wasn't at home already was because I'd called Quadir to see if her car was outside. What I didn't expect was to see her caking it up with the next nigga like they had just came from being on a date. Getting in my car, I pulled off and made my way to Ava's house. I already know this was going to be a long night of ass kissing. The reason why I was even late to my date with Ava was because I was spending family time with Kari and Amari.

We had started that back up because we were trying to co-parent with one another.

Earlier today, Amari and me went shopping and Kari tagged along with us. We ended up buying everything that the baby needed in its nursery, including clothes, and I was stacking up on pampers and wipes. I even paid her rent up because she told me that she currently wasn't working. Time slipped by me, mainly, because my phone was dead. When I had finally turned it on, it was damn near eight thirty and I felt like shit, especially after hearing the multiple voicemails Ava had left. The voicemails range from being angry to being really concerned about me and my safety.

When I'd finally reached Ava's house, I saw Quadir sitting on his front porch smoking a blunt. "You know you done fucked up! Ava on a three-way call with Kai and Aubrey, bad mouthing ya dumb ass," Quadir laughed as I walked over to his porch.

"Pass me that shit." I needed a little buzz before dealing with Ava. I already knew Aubrey and Kai had gotten her hyped the fuck up. So, I knew she was going to be on go as soon as I walked through the front door.

"Nigga, why would you stand her up?" Quadir queried.

"You act like I did that shit on purpose. I was making sure Kari and Amari was good. We had family day and I didn't even realize the time until I turn my phone back on. I was putting up the crib and all of the other things we got the baby." I watch Quadir groan under his breath. He hated that I was going all out for Kari even after the foul shit she'd done to me, but it wasn't for him to understand my actions.

"You don't know if that baby even yours, and you out here shopping and doing the most for this bitch. I swear you and Rashawn been on some fuck shit lately."

"Fuck you, Quadir! Don't worry about my situation. It doesn't have shit to do with you," I snapped at his ass.

"It has everything to do with me when your problems are

interrupting my life. I was damn near balls deep in Kai when Ava call to have a, *I hate men*, session on the fucking phone. You and that nigga Rashawn need to get yall shit together. I'm tired of yall women calling my girl with yall problems. Than Kai getting mad at me because I'm related to yall dumb asses. I swear, if I don't get none tonight I'm fucking you up!"

"Whatever," I chuckled. All Quadir needed was some pussy then his grumpy ass would be back to normal. "I'm about to head on over there." Quadir just nodded his head and continued smoking his weed. Walking over to Ava's house, I headed inside and could hear her talking mad shit about me to her sisters.

"I swear yall, I'm fucking done! I already know he was with his babymama because he told me that he was dropping Amari off to her."

"Pick up and drop off don't take no damn three plus hours or whatever bullshit they called themselves doing," Aubrey fussed. "All I'm saying sis, don't put nothing pass that situation. Next thing you know, he'll be sleeping with a fucking prostitute."

"Bitchhhhhhh... I still can't believe that was the type time Rashawn was on," Ava dragged out her words, being dramatic.

"Well, from what I was told he didn't know she was into that kind of shit. He thought she was just a stripper." Kai always had the voice of reasons.

"Kai, do you not get the concept of men bashing conversation," Aubrey asked, causing Ava to laugh. I felt like a whole creep, eavesdropping on their conversation.

"Well, bitch, I ain't having problems with my man. Shit, before yall called me I was ready to get dick down. "

"Hoe, ya six weeks not even up! You better hope that nigga don't knock ya ass up with some twins or triplets," Ava teased "But for real, I'm trying to be the supportive girlfriend and shit but it's not going to last long if things like this keep happening.

"Ava, get off the phone!" I made my presence known, almost

causing her to jump out her skin.

"Bishhhhh, you heard him! Hey Nasir," Kai said, laughing before Ava could hang up the phone.

"Why are you here, Nasir?" Ava then asked in defeat. The look on her face had me fucked up, and after hearing everything that she said had me annoyed with my damn self.

"I'm sorry," I apologized, but by the look on her face I could tell she wasn't feeling it.

"Where were you and why didn't you have the decency to call and let me know you couldn't make it? That was so inconsiderate of you when it came to me and my time," Ava fussed, now off the phone and had started taking off her clothes.

"I know, but I got caught up. Yesterday I had everything planned out but time just got away from me. Kari and me started the family thing again for Amari's sake, and after we went shopping and everything, I started putting up the crib and swing set that we bought for the baby. I didn't even realize the time because my phone was dead."

"I knew you was with her! Why do you have to spend family time together? Like, Amari is at the age that he can understand that his parents are not together. I'm not trying to tell you how to parent, but Amari is with you during the week, so why Kari just can't keep him for the weekend, without your damn supervision. It's not like he used to seeing yall together anyway. Yall both just came into his life this year. It's not a big difference."

"My situation with Kari has nothing to do with you!" I shot back but instantly regretted it. I knew I was putting Ava in a fucked up position asking her to stand by me while I have a baby with my ex. Granted, when Kari got pregnant I wasn't with her, but I knew she didn't trust me around Kari.

"You're right, I have nothing to do with you guys parenting," she said before grabbing her towel and walked out her room, heading to the bathroom to take a shower. I knew Ava was right, but I wanted to give Amari a feeling of having both parents and a family. "You know what?" Ava busted back through the bedroom door. "Fuck this relationship, especially if you can't see that what happened today should have never happened. I understand co-parenting very well. Yes, there are some things that you and Kari need to do together like holidays, birthday celebration, doctors appointment and thing of that nature, but just spending time together as one big happy fucking family, you might as well go be with the bitch." She was beyond pissed as she huffed and puffed, looking at me with the most irritated expression.

Even though she was mad, she looked good standing in front of me with nothing but a towel wrapped around her body. Standing up, I made my way into her personal space. I could smell the coco butter body wash she used and there were still beads of water covering her body.

"So, its fuck this relationship, huh?" I asked, leaning down to kiss the side of her neck.

"Nasir, stop!" She fought hard trying not to let a moan escape her lips, but I knew Ava's body like the back of my hand. So her trying to fight back the feel I was causing her body was the inevitable.

"Ava, I'm sorry. I know I'm asking a lot of you, I know you're trying and I appreciate your effort. What happened tonight will never happen again," I said, picking her up and placing her on the dresser. She didn't respond but I could see her attitude slowly but surely leaving. I unwrapped her towel and allowed it to fall to the floor.

She now was sitting in front of me as naked as the day she was born. Her smooth chocolate skin looked so radiant. Leaning over, I started to lead a trail of kisses down her body.

"Babe, you forgive me?" I muttered while biting softly on her inner thigh. Ava remained stubborn by ignoring my question. However, she made sure to spread her legs a little farther apart, giving me access to her sweet nectar. I secured her legs into the crook of my arms, causing her to lean her back against the dresser mirror. I started kissing, licking, and sucking the soul out of her pussy.

Tonight, I was on a mission. A mission to get back into my baby's good gracious.

"Fuck," she groaned as I felt her fingers running through and pulling on my dreads. "Make me cum!" She then started grinding her center into my face. I felt her clit pulsate as my tongue caressed it.

"Let that shit go!" I demanded, and on my commanded she erupted.

"Nassssirrrrrrr!" she screamed as her juices started to pour out. I continued to lick and suck until I had every last drop in my mouth. I'd never ate as much pussy as I did now that I'd met Ava. Her scent and her taste were my addiction.

"Damn, ma, you forgive me now?" I asked leading a trail of kisses back up her body. Grabbing the back of her neck, I pulled her into me, pressing my lips against herd and kissing her deeply. All she could was summit to me. "Answer my question."

"No, you didn't earn my forgiveness, yet," she smirked, trying to push me away, but I didn't budge. Ava could play all she wanted but she just didn't even know I was about to stroke her down with this ten-inch dick.

Pulling my shirt over my head, I dropped my jeans and draws. I watched as her eyes roamed all over my body. Picking her up, her arms was wrapped around my neck and her legs were back into the crooks of my arms, pinning her against one of the bedroom wall. I took my time sliding inside of her.

"Shit," I groaned, biting down on her shoulder to keep from moaning like a little bitch, as her pussy walls grip my dick and her juices poured all over me.

Ever since our trip we hadn't been using any condoms. I swear, if she didn't have the birth control implant in her arm, she would have been pregnant by now. But, there's no rush. Not saying I didn't want her to have my kids, I just respected her enough not to get her pregnant the same time I have some one else pregnant. Plus, by the time we had kids, I planned on her having my last name.

"Oh... my...god" Ava moaned, rocking her hips to meet my every thrust. I felt her nails digging and scratching my back as I went as deep as I could. "I'm cumming.... Baby, I forgive you!"

I placed her down on her bed after I felt her body shake in pure ecstasy. I was allowing her some time to get herself together. Laying her flat on her stomach, I slap her hard as hell on her ass.

"Ouch!" Ava yelled but did exactly what I wanted her to do. She got on all four. Ass up and face down just the way I liked it. The way her back was arched and her ass was in the air gave me the perfect view of her pussy. It was soak and wet, waiting with anticipation. The view alone made me harder than I already was, if that was even possible.

"Shut up," I muttered and rammed my dick in her with so much force that she damn near slid across the bed.

"What the fuck?" She moaned as I continued to move in and out of her wet tunnel. These weren't the slow sensual strokes I was giving her before. These were forceful long strokes, making sure I was tapping her cervix which each one. Her smiling in some nigga's face wasn't forgiven. Ava wanted to keep playing with me. She already knew I was about knock bul head off with the way she quickly diffuses the situation.

"Ava, stop fucking with me!" I said as I pounded into her. I could tell she was about to cum by the way her pussy muscles were contracting around my dick. "You not going to be happy until I fuck some shit up!"

"Nassirrrrrr..." Pulling out, I saw her juices coated all over my dick. When I slid back inside, she tried to push me away.

"Naw, take this dick!" I groaned as I placed both of her hands behind her back.

"You... are so deep." She was complaining, moaning and throwing her ass back. Ava didn't know whether to run from the dick or take it like a champ. I swear she had the best pussy ever. Shit was so good I was ready to murk any nigga trying to get close to it.

"Damn, ma," I groaned through gritted teeth. I could feel my nut building up.

"Daddy, cum with me," Ava begged as her body started to shake. With that, I let lose inside her womb. After that release, all you could hear was both of us trying to catch our breaths.

"Stop threatening to leave! You and I both know you're not going anywhere."

"Nigga, don't get cocky because you just got finished slinging that bomb ass dick that had me cumming back to back. Mark my words, I played the fool once but I will never do it again."

"You don't have to worry about that. You're the number one woman in my life and I need you to be confident about your position."

"I'm not insecure and the only way for me to be confident in my position in your life is by your actions, and right now, you're off to a bad start."

"I'm making up for it right now," I said as I pulled her on top of me, ready for round two. I already knew I had a lot of making up to do, and why not start off by long stroking her into complete bliss.

Chapter 16

Rashawn

Two Months Later...

"Wassup Anthony?" I spoke, giving him a pound. Today me, Nasir and Quadir was helping him move all of my mom's things into his house. I was surprised that Rita had agreed to move, especially after all the fighting she had to do to keep the house she shared with my sperm donor.

"Wassup yall? Rashawn, ride with me. Twins, yall can take the U-Haul," Anthony ordered, throwing Nasir the keys. They hopped into the truck and pulled off, heading to my mother's house. I hopped into his Escalade and he pulled off right behind Nasir.

"You sure you want Rita's crazy ass to live with you?" I asked jokingly. I was happy to see my mom happy. And Anthony wasn't a bad person either.

"Yeah!" He said with so much excitement that all I could do was chuckle. "I had plans of making her my wife." Anthony pointed to the glove compartment and motioned for me to open it. Inside was a black velvet box. Taking it out, I opened it to see a diamond and sapphire engagement ring.

"Damn, you really love my mom?" I muttered. The ring was beautiful.

"Yeah, she should have never gotten away the first time. Now that I have my second chance, I'm making sure she'll never get away again. I was young and dumb and we was both too stubborn to fix what was broken, but we're older now and we're ready to take that step."

I respected everything that he said and it had me kind of reflecting back on my situation with Aubrey. Still to this day, Aubrey wasn't feeling me and honestly I was about ready to give up. I knew it was my fault that we were where we're at now but it seemed to me that she didn't even want to make things work. I'd never been a begging nigga and I wasn't about to start with her. No matter how much I loved her I was about ready to let her go.

"What's going on with you and your lady? Have yall made things right?" Anthony then asked and all I could do was shake my head.

"Naw. She seem like she's really set on us not being together." Aubrey's ignorant ass still didn't allow me to sleep in our bedroom. She made me so mad one night that I found all of her little sex toys and vibrators and threw them bitches in the trash. She's out here getting herself off with fake dicks while my real dick was dryer than the Sahara dessert. Fuck that. If I was on a drought, so was she. Aubrey thought I was playing. Just last night I had tied her hand to one of the bars on our headboard because I had walked in and caught her pleasuring herself with her hands.

"I think she's just really hurt. From what your mom tells me you were flaunting the girl like *she* was your fiancée."

"I wasn't taking the bitch out or anything like that. I just had her meet me some places. The most people seen me with her was at her damn job. I know I was wrong but I wasn't about to be out here on some Keith Sweat shit begging and pleading. I apologized and now that should be the end of it. She knows and I know I'm not about to mess up again and risk losing my family."

"Are you serious? Is that your way of thinking," Anthony chuckled, shaking his head. I don't know why he even asked me that question. Everything I said seemed to make perfect sense to me.

"Yeah!"

"Rashawn, you can't rush her feelings. She doesn't know that you will never cheat on her again. I'm pretty sure she didn't think you would do it this time. Not only did you cheat you started neglecting your family, and regardless if you think it wasn't over a chick, to Aubrey it will be because of that girl. On top of that, you're forcing yourself on her. You're not giving her an option to choose and that right there is going to push Aubrey farther away from you." As irritating as it was, I saw where he was coming from. "Sometimes it's just to let go than if it meant to be than it will be."

"Yeah, you're right. I'm just not trying to see her with another nigga. I almost killed the last one she was with," I admitted truthfully. The only reason why the nigga Morgan was alive was because he saved Aubrey's life. That little fact alone would haunt me for the rest of my life. I felt like I failed her. Now Cinnamon's dumb ass, she was in the wind. I couldn't wait to catch up with that bitch. I didn't know what was wrong with these bitches coming for my child, but Cinnamon's days were numbered.

"You lost the option when you were out here doing you. That should have been the thought that stopped you from cheating." I swear I was about to punch Anthony in the damn face. I knew everything he was saying was true but a nigga didn't want to keep hearing that.

"But what I really need to talk to you about is my partner Rossi. He and ole girl is in cahoots."

"Yo', I don't even know why your partner have a hard on for me. I swear I never seen him a day in my life accept when he came to investigate the wedding shooting."

"Rossi, have it out for you bad, and it's personal on his end. Last week your mom and me went to the annual Philadelphia Police vs. Philadelphia Fire Fighters basketball game tournament and while we were there, the some lady came up yelling at your mom, talking about her son was a murder. When I went to where the commotion was, it was Rossi's ex-wife. Come to find out their son is the one who attempted to rob you."

"I didn't kill that nigga! So, why the fuck she is calling me a murder," I snapped, and he chuckled

"Ya' mom said that same thing," he said, shaking his head. "But he committed suicide a couple of months before your wedding."

Shaking my head, I remembered that night like it was yesterday. I was leaving my mom's house with Kylie when this white boy caught me slipping, holding me at gunpoint. I knew exactly who he was. He was one of my customers. His name was Kevin Rossi, a hardcore heroine user.

That night he was currently in debt to me and I wouldn't supply him with anything until I got my money. He was usually good with payments, but his had family cut him off financially, thinking it would stop his drug habit. Not realizing all it did was caused him to do the unthinkable and started robbing people. That night he decided to rob his supplier. I was so mad that he'd caught me slipping and I had Kylie with me. I knew my only choice was to shoot him. I could tell Kevin was nervous by the way his hand was shaking and I knew his aim would've been off had he would've fired a shot. I couldn't risk him shooting Kylie, and I much rather had done jail time than bury my daughter.

"So, how is he connected to Cinnamon?" I asked.

"Well, like he admitted, he'd been watching you on his time off and I've been following him. I saw him come to Jasmine's house a couple of times but she never answered the door for him. I believe she was in town. Then my man, Jeff, he too a police officer but G.M.M have him on their payroll and came to me saying that Jasmine gave up information on the trap houses she visited you at. Jeff came to me because he knows your mom is my woman. So he was giving me a fair warning before he went to G.M.M. Rossi is putting together a task force along with the Captain. They're trying to keep me out of the loop because it's a conflict of interest."

"Who the fuck is Jasmine, and a nigga just got out of jail, so why the fuck the Captain coming for me?" I was beyond frustrated at this point. I figured Jasmine was Cinnamon, but I had to be sure about it.

"Like I told you earlier, Rossi its personal. He feels like with you gone he'd revenged his son's death, even though Kevin committed suicide. Now as for the Captain, you're just a piece in his game of chess. You're second in command to G.M.M, you're right underneath the leaders. To be honest, Angelo and Cream is just casualties of the war. He want the Black Brothers and the connect, Ghost. Yall are just disposable people to him. However, he could never get close enough to G.M.M.

"G.M.M. soldiers are trained to die before dishonor. They will never snitch. That's punishable by death and if you try to run they come for your family. Now, who the fuck is Jasmine?" I stared at him, waiting for him to confirm what I already knew.

"Jasmine is the stripper chick. Son, I need you to know who you sticking ya dick in and messing up your family for," Anthony said with so much disappointment in his tone.

"Shit, I didn't know the hoe name."

"That's what makes this even worse."

I couldn't even say nothing smart because I totally agreed with him. Hearing Cinnamon had loose lips had me seeing red. Good thing Angelo and Cream made us change our trap house location every three weeks and sold the houses that we had over a year. The two I took cinnamon to, we no longer used. Angelo had actually sold them last month. So, if Philly P.D decided to bust in there, they would have a lot of explaining to do busting down somebody else's door. Our trap houses looked like a regular family's four to five bedrooms home. They weren't even in the hood or anything, and were spread out around Philadelphia middle class neighborhoods.

"I don't have anything to worry about. The two houses she knew about have now been sold, but I'll make sure Lo and Cream switch things around just to be on the safe side."

I was pulling rookie ass mistakes. Now I have to explain to

these niggas why the traps have to switch again, when we'd just switched them last week. I was drawling, shitting where I ate. Bitter females were the main reason for a street nigga downfall.

The rest of the ride was in silence except for the phone call I made on my burner phone to let Angelo and Cream know what was going on.

"Officer Jenkins." Rita sang switching over to him as we got out of the car.

"Hey baby." He kissed, and I unintentionally turn my nose up.

"Wassup trick?" My mom's disrespectful ass acknowledged my presence, causing Nasir and Quadir to laugh.

"Mom, chill." I waved her off. I wasn't in the mood for her shenanigans.

"No, I'm not going to chill. You know Ronnie's bigheaded ass ran her mouth. Talking about the girl in the sex tape is a prostitute and according to Aubrey, you were throwing this girl money right and left."

"Rita, he's not here for a damn lecture!" Anthony snapped on my mom, shutting her right on up and ending her bashing session. I never seen someone shut my mom up before. Her mouth was one of the reasons why my dad used to beat her ass on the regular. "Did you finish packing?"

"Yes, and I see you trying to save him from my tongue lashing."

"Yeah, because this situation has nothing to do with you or anyone else." I never thought I would ever fuck with a cop, but Anthony was earning all of my respect.

"Well, I want him to know he needs to do better. Rashawn, if you can't be responsible and be the man I raised you to be and be the man you want for your daughter to marry, then I would advise you to leave Aubrey alone. To be honest, she deserves better than you. I'm not saying she's perfect because God knows she have some shit with her too, but no woman should be put through what you put her through. You weren't in the clinic with her scared out her mind as she got tested for every possible STD there is," my mom said before walking back into her house.

I knew she was upset. She watched me dog girls after girls even though I knew the heartbreak it would bring them, and I even watched my father do my mom dirty on many occasions. Thinking about it, I hated to admit but maybe I wasn't the man for Aubrey.

Even if I tried to be, which I was currently doing, my past sins seemed to have been too much for her to move forward from. At this point, I didn't deserve Aubrey. What type of nigga was I to have my girl up in the clinic because I was out here fucking around on her with any and everything? It was obvious that I didn't have any pick fucking with Cinnamon streetwalking ass. Aubrey should have never been put in that situation.

Chapter 17

Quadir

"Yo' Kasim, wassup with you? You've been walking around here looking all depressed and shit. Turning away customers and missing appointments," I said, walking into Kasim's tattoo room that he rented out from me. Kasim was losing money and that wasn't the kind a business I was running.

"Qua, so much shit been going on with me on a personal level." He stated, taking a seat in his chair. I could see the stress line forming on his forehead. Whatever he was going through was seriously taking a toll on him.

"Wassup, what's going on?" This heart to heart thing wasn't me, but I was the boss and I wanted all of my employees to feel comfortable enough to come to me with any issues they were having, especially if it was effecting their work ethic.

"So, I don't know if you know, but my girl is pregnant," he blurted out and his confession took me by surprise. I didn't even know this nigga had a girl. He damn near fucked every single one of his female customers. Just last week, two bitches were fighting each other over him.

"Nigga, where this girl at? You keeping her a secret and shit?"

"It's not that I was keeping her a secret, I just know you don't fuck with her." I stared at him with the confused look. I wasn't one of those men who got into it with bitches, and I never cared if someone was smashing on of my dips[A53]. I never took them seriously anyways. Kai was honestly the only woman who had ever my heart.

"Who is she?" I asked, looking at him, and the way her was looking all nervous had me ready to rock this shit out of him. I was trying to be patient but I had a feeling he was about to say some foul shit.

"My girl was, Sharonda," he confessed, looking me dead in the eyes. "I know you didn't fuck with her because of the Trinity and Kai situation. So I made sure to never bring her around." In one quick motion, I had Kasim gripped fuck knocking down at of his equipment and tools.[A54]

"Did you know what the fuck that bitch was doing to my girl while she was in that coma?" I barked, causing him to flinch. If he didn't start explaining himself soon, I was going to break his face in with my bare hands.

"No! No!" he screamed and I slowly let him go. "Quadir, you know me better than that. I didn't even know she was doing that crazy shit until I saw her face plastered all over the news. Sharonda and me had already broke up with she was keeping her loyalty to that girl Trinity. [A55]I knew she knew where Trinity was. I even asked for her info but she stayed loyal to her friend. Regardless of everything, Kai didn't deserve what they did to her." I could tell he was being sincere with every word he spoke. Throughout the months, Kai became very close to everybody that worked in my shop. We're all like a family and when me and Kai got serious, they considered her family too.

"Qua, you're like my brother. I will always be loyal to you. I don't even care about Sharonda after the foul shit she pulled. Don't get me wrong, I loved shorty, but I couldn't rock with how she was rolling. If she drugged Kai while she was in that coma, I can only imagine what she would do to my ass if I fucked up and broke her heart or some shit. I would obviously be on the next episode of Snapped. I only care about my seed she's carrying."

Damn. I thought, shaking my head. That bitch was never coming back. I wasn't going to lie, I thought Sharonda was lying when she screamed out she was pregnant. But after we drowned her, we place her body in the acid and by the time I pulled her out, her stomach was wide opened and I saw her fetus. Well, what was left of it. Her killing fucked me up for a little bit. Mainly because of the baby she was carrying. That was a cruel way to kill a baby. But I justify my actions by looking at this situation as, an eye for an eye. It was fucked up but she should have thought about her unborn child before she fucked with mine.

"So, she just got ghost on you, huh?" I asked with a straight face, playing dumb.

"Yeah, before everything blew up in her face she was calling and texting me non-stop. Then the day everything came out on the news, she went missing. No one heard from her since then. I know the police is looking for her. I think she's on the run, even her mother haven't heard from her."

"I'm pretty sure she'll pop up," was all I could get out before my receptionist walked into the room.

"Quadir, someone is asking for you in the front," Tyesha said, rolling her eyes at Kasim. I didn't even know how Tyesha got caught up with him, but she was head over heels for that nigga.

"Kasim, if you need to take some time off go head, but if you working I need you to be on you're A game."

Walking towards the front of the shop, I was caught off guard seeing Rhonda sitting in my waiting area. I knew she was bound to pop up sooner or later. After I cut off all ties with her, she started blowing up my phones like crazy. Every time I blocked one of her numbers she was calling back with another one. I wasn't about to cause unnecessary drama in my relationship with Kai, so I changed my number and the shop's number. Not only did I block her from calling me, I blocked her from all of me and the shop's social media accounts. Looking at the ceiling, I tried to calm myself down. Thinking to myself, I was happy as hell Kai decided to start going back to work. The last thing I needed her to see was one of my old hoes in my face. I was originally mad that she started working again, but she loved her job and like she said, it was nothing like making your own money.

"What are you doing here?" I asked, looking at her sitting down reading a magazine like she belonged in my shop.

"Hey babe." Rhonda perked up, hearing my voice.

"Bitch, correct yourself." Tyesha snapped before I could say anything. Tyesha ad Kai had become came close. So it was nothing to Tyesha to put females in their place when Kai wasn't here to do it herself.

"Shouldn't you be doing your job, answering phones and making appointments or some shit like that," Rhonda screamed.

"Hoe, you tried it with your IT the clown looking ass. All that fucking makeup caked on your ugly ass face," Tyesha pointed out, walking around her receptionist desk.

"Chill, we're not doing this in my shop!" I said, giving Tyesha a look that said calm the fuck down. I had this situation handled. Just a couple of weeks ago I had Kasim bitches trying to tear my shit up, and I definitely wasn't trying to have a repeat of that craziness.

"Quadir, can we go in your office to talk in private?"

"Naw, right here is fine! Plus, you're about leave. I told you the best way that I could the night at Buffalo Wild Wings that me and my girl are back together, and I have a child..."

"Okayyyy," Rhonda cut me off, dragging out her words in an uninterested tone. "I didn't come here for that. I came here to let you know I need to be in contact with you because your about to have baby number two." Standing up, I could see what could be a baby bump.

"Errrrrr," Tyesha said, making a noise that sounded like Scooby Doo, snapping her neck in my directions.

"I'll never get a hoe like you pregnant. You're the same bitch that sucked my dick in the car after I fucked the shit out of my babymama at the restaurant."

"How special can she be to you to have me suck your dick? Obviously, she wasn't handling her business," she barked in a matter of fact tone, like her actions was acceptable.

"She's my heart and one day soon to be my wife. I would never allow her to suck the juices of another bitch pussy after I was done fucking someone else."

"So, bitch, that alone should let you know how special you are cum bucket." Tyesha had to add her two cents.

All I could do was laugh.

"Whatever." Rhonda rolled her eyes and had the nerve to rub her stomach.

"How are you pregnant by me when I strapped up every time and pulled out when I busted, and when you gave me head I made sure you swallowed?"

"That's where you're wrong baby daddy. There were plenty a time my head had you so far gone that you didn't take your extra ridiculous precautions." Now I was confused because when could a bitch ever get pregnant by giving head. "I see the look of confusion on your face. So, let me explain. The night you didn't check to make sure I swallowed, I spit everything you gave me into a turkey baser. I tracked my cycle and when I made sure to shoot your sperm [A56]up in right before I was ovulating to make sure I would get pregnant."

"Damn," I heard people that were in the shop whisper.

"Oh, I see you a calculating bitch. It's never that serious to trap a nigga, and you decide to trap the undercover psychopath." Tyesha mumbled right before I gripped Rhonda up by the neck and pushed her against the wall. Today was the day I killed a bitch in from of my employees. As fucked up as it may have sound, her and this baby was about to die. I wasn't about to be in Mikey shoes. Kai would never forgive me. Even though I had never messed with this girl while we were together, I knew this situation was too similar to hers and Mikey's.

"Everybody leave!" I heard George and Kasim demanding to every customer and leading them to the door.

Click

"Fuck," Tyesha mumbled, as she took cover behind the counter and everybody else stood frozen as they heard my gun cock back. Rhonda was standing in front of me with tears rolling down her face, messing up her make up.

"So you called yourself trapping me?" I asked and let out a chuckle. I never truly wanted my employees to see this side of me. I let off a shot right by her head causing her to scream.

"Oh my god... please, I'm lying." Rhonda yelled, pulling up her shirt, showing me and everybody that she had on one of those fake pregnancy bellies. I couldn't believe this hoe truly went this far. "It's fake, please don't kill me," she then begged.

"I'm going to tell you this one last time, stay the fuck away from me and my girl! If you see us walking down the street, you better cross to the other side. Act like you never knew me, let alone stuck my dick down your throat," I hissed through gritted teeth. I hated females like Rhonda. Bitches like her were the main reason why some kids today were fatherless. Trapping men with kids was only setting themselves and the kid up for failure, especially if the nigga didn't want to be a father. Respect to the ones who still took care of their kids after finding out their babymama trapped them or worse, found out years later that the child was not theirs.

"I'm sorry." Rhonda was doing her ugly cry with snot bubbles coming out her nose.

"See, you almost lost your life being a dumb bitch!" Tyesha said, finally standing up from her hiding place.

"Get the fuck out of here!" George roared, snatching Rhonda up and damn near throwing her out the front door.

"Yall get back to work and tell yall nosey ass client to stop peeking in my damn windows. Make sure you give them a discount for their pieces after seeing that bullshit. I'll pay yall the difference," I said before walking back to my office I had a damn headache.

"Yo', Quadir, can I talk to you?" Kasim asked, knocking on my door[A57].

"Wassup?"

"After seeing everything that just went down, I know you won't hesitate to kill for Kai. I know you have to be looking for Sharonda, especially after drugging Kai while she was pregnant. So, I'm asking you, please don't kill Sharonda She's pregnant with my child." His words came out nervously, and I could see the emotions on his face, and my man was hurt over this girl.

It made me feel a little guilty.

"Trust me, I haven't found her." I lied with a straight face as my head shook. Boys or not, I was never admitting I taking his girl's life. "But would I be wrong to kill the girl who brought harm to my girl and child? Sharonda didn't think about herself or her child when she came for mine."

"I understand and I know I'm putting you in a hard position, but as a man I know you have to protect you family by any means necessary and you're right Sharonda didn't think of our child or herself playing with other people lives. I just asking you if you find her, keep my child alive. I don't care what you do to her. Like I said earlier, I can never get down with how she moves."

"I hear you, but like a said, she's been ghost and it's probably best she stay that way." That was the end of the conversation and Kasim caught the hint. I would keep my eyes on him for now but Kasim was a hood nigga, he knew the consequences of Sharonda's actions. It was evitable.

"Hello," I answer my phone for Kai. [A58]

"Hey baby! Guess what?" She sounded so excited. I swear I could picture her short ass smiling, showing all her pearly whites.

"What?"

"The NIC- Unit called and they said Miracle can come home." I could hear her crying but I knew it was tears of joy. These pass couple of months with Miracle in the NIC-Unit was hard. I'd been a praying man asking God to bring my baby girl home and now my prayers were finally being answered. She had been passing tests after tests and so far there are no disabilities that they'd come across and I was praying that she would never have any.

"That's wassup! Where you at now?" As I was asking that, I was grabbing my keys and making my way out of my office. "Tyesha, lock uo for me tonight and you're probably going to be opening for the rest of the week." I let her know and she nodded her head,

"I'm on my way home. Meet me there so we can drive to-gether."

"I told you my baby girl was strong. She's leaving the hospital before they thought she would."

"I know, babe, and you have no idea how happy I am. And, Quadir, I love you so much. Thank you for being that man that needed you to be," Kai professed her love before hanging up. I swear that girl was my heart. Words couldn't even explain my feelings for her. I had to make her my wife ASAP. She meant too much to me just to be my girlfriend/babymama. I needed her as my wife!

Chapter 18

Jasmine (Cinnamon)

"Bye, mom, I'll call you as soon as I get home," I yelled over my shoulder before walking out my mother's front door.

I had been staying with my mother ever since that whole mall fiasco. I knew as soon as Rashawn's babymama told him that I had put hands on his daughter, it was off with my head. When my girlfriend, Cherry, from the strip club told me that Rashawn's crew had been up in the club, I didn't think too much about it. It wasn't a time when G.M.M wasn't having a party at KINGS. It wasn't until she told me that they were looking for me personally, that I knew I had to stay in Maryland to escape Rashawn's wrath.

In the beginning of me and Rashawn's situation, I was happy as hell Kari had put me on. That man had me paid. I didn't know when he put us on to Snake that he was literally a pimp. He was taking damn near all of our money and beating our ass if we were short.

Rashawn was giving me enough money to give my cut to Snake and have money left over on top of what I was making at KINGS. I wasn't out here like Kari and the rest of the girls, including Kari pill popping mother, sleeping with any and everybody. I think that's why I fell for Rashawn because unbeknownst to him he was keeping me out a bad situation. Kari really screwed us over and the only reason why Snake fell back off of the girls was because they'd told our boss King Black, and he made a visit to Snake.

Next thing I knew, Snake stopped messing with all of the girls that still worked a KINGs.

I knew Rashawn didn't care for me. He didn't even know my real name and didn't even bother to ask. All I was to him was somebody to keep his mind off his problems at home and to be honest, it probably wasn't him that I'd fallen for. It was more so of his money. So seeing his girl and daughter in the Gucci store had me pissed. I was dead broke. Like, I was jealous of their daughter. Why were they buying her little ass Gucci, anyway? Seeing them walk around like a happy little family got under my skin, especially when he was pillow talking with me about how much of a nag Aubrey was.

I didn't mean for my pettiness to turn into this big situation. I just wanted to cause some disorder in their lives because his crazy ass had me hiding out like a thief in the night. I was fired from KINGs for too many call outs. The only reason why I was living at my mom's house was because my landlord was evicting me, and I still needed to get my clothes. Also, because Officer Rossi had reached out to me asking for any information to put Rashawn behind bars. I was happy to give him all the information about the trap houses I used to visit him at, but it had been two months and Officer Rossi still hadn't made an arrest.

According to Cherry, Rashawn was still out in the streets of Philly, flooding them with drugs with G.M.M.

Picking up my phone, I called Officer Rossi. The least he could do was make sure I was safe as I went to get my clothes from my house. I needed to be in and out without being seen. I could only imagine what Rashawn had in stores for me. He already had gotten me jumped by his sister and her gay ass friends all because he thought I had told his girlfriend about our situation and was trying to blackmail him, and that was just base off his assumption.

Now back to the day at the mall, even though I had only pushed the little brat, I knew he probably wanted to kill me. Hopefully he hadn't gotten word about me setting him up.

"Hello," Officer Rossi answered, sounding like his fat ass was eating a donut.

"Hey, this is Jasmine." I said, and heard him sigh loud like I was bothering him.

"I'm on lunch. What do you need?" He had the nerve to say, like I wasn't hiding out from a crazy ass nigga who wasn't all the way there mentally.

"I'm on my way back to Philly because I need to get my belongings from my house, and I was wondering if you could meet me over there. Rashawn have been looking for me and I need some protection."

"Relax. By the time you get here, there would be a task force busting down all of his trap houses you told us about. That nigger won't have time to come looking for you," he informed me before hanging up in my face. I was slightly offended for the simple fact that he thought it was okay for him to use the N word like he wasn't white. Yet, on the other hand, I was happy he was finally doing something with the information that I was really risking my life to give to him.

Honestly, after I got my clothes I was never returning back to Philly. Snitching on Rashawn was snitching on G.M.M, the most feared gang in Philly, and that was an automatic death sentence.

It took me about two hours to return to Philly and my landlord was waiting for me.

"Jasmine, you finally decided to show your face?" My landlord fussed as soon as I got out of the car.

"Yes, and I'm sorry about everything. It's just; my life has been twisted upside down lately. I promise I will get you your money, though," I explained while walking up the steps.

"There's no need because I'm about to receive a payment now." When he uttered that, I wanted to question him on what he meant, but I thought it was nothing so I didn't bothered. He opened the door and when we walked inside, I felt the piss trickled down my legs. Looking back at my landlord, I could tell he was filled with regret because he'd just set me up for my death.

Sitting on the couch smoking blunts was Rashawn, Angelo, and Cream. I already knew Rashawn wasn't all the way there in the head, and I used to hear the gruesome stories of how Cream and Angelo would kill the people who did them dirty. G.M.M didn't have picks. They would come for men, women, old people and even kids.

They were beyond ruthless.

"Wassup, Cinnamon?" Rashawn spoke so cordially that you wouldn't have even believed I was probably in my last hours of life. I decided not to say anything. I couldn't even speak if I wanted to being that I was filled up with nothing but fear. I knew they could see me trembling. "Damn, you can't speak? You acting like you didn't always have my dick in your mouth."

Cream and Angelo bust out laughing and so did my landlord, with his bitch ass. I swear if I weren't so scared I would've cussed Rashawn's dumb ass out. My life was so fucked up I didn't even know why I'd decided to approach Rashawn's babymama.

I should have just left well enough alone when I had a chance to do so.

"So I'm going to get out of yall's hair. Am I getting paid now you yall find me later?" My landlord's greedy ass said with his hand out. Cream looked at Angelo then Rashawn before letting out a chuckle. He then stood up and dug in his back pocket.

"Yeah, come here," Angelo commanded. Rick, my landlord's happy go lucky ass walked over to Angelo like he wasn't handed me my death on silver platter. In one quick motion, Angelo whipped out a pocketknife and stabbed him right in the side of the neck.

"Dammmn!" Rashawn yelled. Now I officially knew I was going to die. My landlord's blood was spraying everywhere as I watched him fall to the ground, choking on his own blood.

"Lo, I thought you was really going to pay him." Cream shook his head before pulling out his phone and started texting on it.

"Fuck him! He's weak and stupid. Like, why on Gods green earth would he think I would allow him to live after he lured this rat bitch to me? If you're not G.M.M, I don't trust you."

"So you thought it was okay to put your hands on my daughter?" Rashawn inquired, focusing his attention back on me.

"Rashawn, I didn't mean too. It was just a reaction. Her mom and me were fighting and your daughter tripped me, giving your baby mama the advantage. To be truthful, they jumped me." I knew I was reaching with my statement and the looks on their faces told me they felt it too.

"Bitch, are you serious?" Cream was laughing so hard that his light skinned ass was turning red.

"Not only did you touch my child because she was riding for her mother, who you had no business even confronting, from what I hear you was being petty and Aubrey molly wopped you upside ya damn head for coming to her with the bullshit in front of our daughter, but you decided to turn rat too"

Fuck!

"You know ratting is punishable by death." Cream said in a calm smooth voice that sent chills up my spine.

"Please, I didn't turn rat. I will never do that to you, Rashawn, or to G.M.M," I tried pleading my case and pleading for my life. I prayed that Rossi got off his fat ass and came bussing through that door. I swear I should have never allowed his fat ass to persuade me to snitch on Rashawn. I was just so angry that he had his sister and her friends to jump me. Then, when he realized he assumed wrong he left without a sorry. He wasn't even man enough to come back and get his things. He had some nigga run in my house to pick up his clothes and shoes.

I watched in fear as Cream and Anglo stalked over to me and grabbed. I fought and scream trying to break free from the grasped but it was to no avail. They tied me down to my dining room chair. I cried so hard not knowing how my death would come.

Rashawn made his way to me with an axe in one hand and butcher knife in the other.

"Please… I'm sorry," I wept as Cream and Angelo both held my arms in front of me, placing them on my glass dining room table. In one swing Rashawn cut off my right hand and followed up with the left.

"Aaaaahhhhhhhh!" I screamed as blood pour profusely from my wrist, and my hands laid on the table beside my body.

"That is for touching my daughter. This is for your loose lips," he said grabbing my face and forcing my mouth open. I had no fight left in me as I was slowly slipping in and out of consciousness. I felt him grab my tongue and pull it out of my mouth against my will. I started panting knowing what was following after he'd done that.

"Loose lips sink ships!" Cream said and Rashawn cut my tongue right out of my mouth with no remorse. Blood instantly began poring out as I slowly drowned in my own blood.

Chapter 19

Officer Rossi

"Rossi, it's time," Captain Anderson announced, patting me on my back.

Today was going to be a good day. We were finally making the move to crack down on G.M.M's operation. Jasmine was just a pawn into bringing down Rashawn. I was willing to bring him down by any means necessary. I didn't care that the way I was going about everything was unethical. My problem with Rashawn Rogers was personal. My son took his own life and that my seem as a personal decision in Kevin's behalf, but I know for a fact Rashawn was the main reason for Kevin untimely death.

Kevin became addicted to drugs in high school. Did you know how embarrassing it was as a cop to have a drug addict as a son? Don't get me wrong, I loved my son and his mother and me did everything in our power to get him clean. When he went to college, he fell off the wagon. I was called plenty of times from the precinct to get Kevin who had managed to get himself caught up in drug raids. Or, if one of my fellow officers recognized him they would call me to pick him up.

My ex-wife used to give Kevin money all the time even though all he did was feed his drug habits. *Me?* I made the hard decision to cut him off in hopes that he would get his life together, but he continued his drug use. I never thought cutting him off would cause him to rob his drug dealer. The night Rashawn shot Kevin was the worst night of my life. No parent should have to endure the anticipation of knowing if their child was going to live or die.

My Justice system, the one I worked for and tried so hard to uphold failed me when they allowed Rashawn to get away with self-defense. He only received jail time because the gun he had was unregistered. That was a slap in the face. I didn't care that Kevin tried to rob him with his daughter in his arms, he knew just like I did Kevin would have never shot him. While Rashawn was in prison Kevin had gotten his life together, but soon as he was let out Kevin became paranoid that Rashawn was going to come back and finish him off. He fell into a deep depression and was slowly but surely losing his sanity.

I always believed that Rashawn was secretly sending silent threats to my son. Kevin's paranoia had gotten so bad that he decided to swallow seven Percocet's, leaving his mother and me a note saying he was finally free and had killed himself before Rashawn could.

Captain Anderson's only motive was to get the drugs off the streets. Taking down the notorious G.M.M would be a great day in the city of Philadelphia. With the help of him, we set a drug task force and we were about to raid the two drug houses that Jasmine had told me about. I couldn't lie, every time we scope out the houses it didn't have much traffic, but I knew she wasn't lying. This was a girl Rashawn had gotten attacked and all I had to do was plant a seed in her head to turn her back on him, but I had to keep my partner Jenkins out of the loop. I could no longer trust him being as though he was sleeping with the bastard's mother.

"We're here! Let's be alert because there is no room for errors. Remember, these men in the house are armed and dangerous. Please protect yourselves and your brothers in blue," Captain stressed to us all. I was so excited I could taste the victory. My adrenaline was pumping as we move closer to the house. Since the judge issued us a no knock warrant, we were taking them totally by surprised. Standing back, I watched the two of my fellow officers knock down the door with the battering ram.

"Go! Go! Go!" I screamed as we all rushed inside, stepping on the knocked down door. All I could hear was screaming as we ran through the house searching everywhere for drugs and guns.

"My Daughter!" A lady screamed, running towards us as she continued to scream like a banshee.

"Stop resisting arrest!" The Captain yelled, tackling her to the ground and placing her hands behind her back.

"Why the fuck yall bust in my house like that?" A man then roared, coming from the back in handcuffs. "Where's Sammy?" I heard the panic in his voice and I was starting to get worried. Actually, taking the time to look at the house it didn't look anything like a trap house. "Where the fuck is my daughter?" After not seeing his daughter in sight, he started fighting our officers to break out of their grasp.

"She's under the door!" The woman exclaimed, and I swear my heart dropped into the pit of my stomach. My men moved into action and packed the door up.

"Noooooo!" The mother let out a gut-wrenching scream and the father started kicking the officers around him. All he wanted to do was get to his daughter, but his aggressive behavior caused us to tase him multiple times to get hold of him.

"I heard one of the officers calling over the radio for an ambulance. The little girl appeared to be no older then two years old and she was lay motionless. I knew for sure we trampled over her coming into this house, and I could smell the civil law suit coming our way.

"Where's the drugs?" I asked. We still had a mission to complete and everybody was at a standstill after finding the little girl.

"Nothing was found in house two." I heard come over the radio that the Captain held in his hand. "Fuck!" Anderson mumbled.

"There's no drugs here we are first time home buyers. We just moved to this house two months ago," she cried and the officers let her go to stand by her child.

"Ma'am, do not touch her. Wait until the ambulance come," Anderson ordered, looking at me with nothing but anger and regret in his eyes. "Rossi!" He then barked my name.

This was a bad look. Neither one of the houses had drugs or illegal firearm in them. I was beyond pissed that I'd just sent my Captain and fellow officers on a complete dummy mission in result of a child being hurt. The last thing polices needed to be was head lining in the Philadelphia inquirer for misconduct.

"Who the hell did you get this information from?" Anderson pulled me to the side. I could hear the paramedics rushing into the house as he spoke.

"I promise you that the information was legit. They must have found out about our plan. Maybe Jenkins said something to them. You know he's dating Rashawn Rogers mother."

"How could Jenkins say anything when he was left out of the loop. This assignment was top secret. Now we have a possible law suit on our hands because of bad information."

"I got the information from Rashawn's side piece," I admitted, and from the look on Andersons face I'd royally fucked up.

"So you telling me you took the word of some girl who had a personal vendetta against him? Girls like that will tell you anything because he cut her off." He said before the ringing of his phone interrupted us. "Hello… alright we'll be there."

"Is everything good?" I asked.

"No! Shit is hitting the fan. The commissioner wants us down at his office now." I was at a lost of words. I was ready to kill Jasmine my damn self. She really played me and I pray that Rashawn caught up to her before me.

"The little girl is alive but is banged up and she have two broken legs." One of the paramedic said. Not only did the little girl need an ambulance, but the father went also because he was having breathing problems after being tase multiple times.

I just wanted this day to be over. This operation was a total fail. I hated the fact that it seemed as Rashawn kept slipping through the cracks. He seemed to have been one step ahead of me every time. He needed to spend the rest of his life in jail and I was the one who was going to make that happen.

Anderson and I went straight to Commissioner Taylor Officer after the raid. Walking to his office I was on pen and needles. I didn't know what to expect, but I knew we were in trouble because he wanted us to come directly to his office.

"Have a seat," was all he said when we walked into the office. What had me confuse was my partner Jenkins standing right beside Commissioner Taylor. "Do anyone of you like to explain why the city of Philadelphia Police Department have a possible lawsuit on our hands?" Captain Anderson looked at me, giving me the look to explain because had he done it, he would certainly throw me under the bus.

"I had some information that turn out to be false. Rashawn Rogers and the whole G.M.M operation had been a menace to the city of Philadelphia for years. I had a lead and I advise the Captain that we go for it. However it seem like they gotten information about our plans because the bust was a complete failure and in the process of the raid, a little girl was badly injured," I explained the best of my ability.

"Rashawn Rogers? Please don't tell me that this is the same Rogers that shot your son."

"Yes it is. Trust me, I have no personal reason to go after Rashawn except that he's second in command to the leaders of G.M.M. G.M.M been our target for so long and we've been trying to bring them down to get closer to the Black brothers. To be honest, he was just a bread crumb in our plan to take down a bigger fish."

"Well, I find that hard to believe that this wasn't personal, especially when your partner has proof of you stalking Rashawn Rogers and his family. It seems more personal than you doing your actual job."

"He killed my son!" I yelled. I didn't understand why they were trying to act like I was in the wrong.

"No, your son committed suicide! Now, as sad as that is, that was a decision Kevin choose to do. You yelling out Rashawn's a murder is not going to bring your son back or any type of justice you think he deserves. Your son was an addict who tried to rob a man at gunpoint, with his child in his arms." Taylor barked. "I need you to turn in your badge and gun. Internal Affair will be starting an investigation on the raid. I have so much damage control to do," he fussed.

I was beyond livid as I handed over my gun and badge.

"Captain Anderson! You may be looking at a demotion within the next couple weeks. How can you allow something like this to happen? Did you do a thorough investigation before getting the warrant for the raid? Or did you decide along with your fellow officer to cut corners think this was going to be a big open and shut case."

"I..." Anderson started but he knew Commissioner Taylor was correct. We cut so many corners that he couldn't even defend himself.

"You're dismissed!" He the stated to me. Getting out of my seat, I knew I was probably as red as a tomato. First stop I was going to make was top Jasmine's house. I knew she said she was stopping by there to get her things and I wanted to catch her before she left. I quickly walked around to the car that me and Anderson rode together in and pulled off. Jasmine better had come up with some information that I could use because now my job was on the line.

Pulling up to Jasmine's house, I could see the light's on. Her front door was unlocking as I made my way inside, I smelt something that I couldn't put my finger on.

"Jasmine!" I called out her names, walking farther into the house. I found her sitting at the dining room table, but the light was off in the room. That should have been a sign for me to back up and leave, but I needed some answered. "You don't here me talking to you." I pushed her, and her body fell onto the floor. Rushing to turning on the lights, the sight in front of me made me throw up my lunch and everything else I had in my stomach.

I looked at her and her hands had been cut off and her mouth on down was covered in blood. Pulling out my gun, I knew Rashawn did this. I made my way to the kitchen and saw another body laying face down.

What the fuck?

"Rossi, is that you?" A voice said from behind me. Turning around, I was face with the grim reaper himself. It was Rashawn dressed in all black.

"I'm calling the police!"

"I thought you were the police? But, you and I both know after that raid you and I both know no ones coming to your aid. Let's play a game of Russian Roulette."

"You're crazy!" I said, shaking my head no.

"Why not? I know you're not bitching up on me?" He reached over, snatching my gun out of my hand and I noticed he had on gloves. I knew that was to make sure he didn't leave any fingerprints behind.

Emptying the gun clip, Rashawn only inserted one bullet back inside the chamber.

"Sit down," he then instructed. "I'll go first."

Taking the gun, he placed it to his head and pulled the trigger. I jumped and he stood still, his breathing didn't even change one bit. It was like he had no fear at all when it came to death. Giving me the gun, I did the same thing, and nothing happened. I silently thanked god. Rashawn pulled the trigger again, and once again nothing happened. It was my time and I was getting nervous.

"Pull the fucking trigger!" He yelled. I didn't want to die. I just wanted to avenge my son's life. Kevin could have been anything I the streets and people like Rashawn didn't get to him.
Feeling as if this was the shot that would send me out, I closed my eyes, said a small prayer and pulled the trigger like I was ordered

to do.

POW!

I felt the bullet penetrate my head and everything went black.

Chapter 20

Ava

"**H**appy Father's Day," I said to Nasir as soon as he walked into my parents' backyard. Every year my mother threw our Rose family annual Father's Day cookout. This day was special because this was Nasir and Quadir's first time celebrating the holiday and the first one Rashawn was celebrating with Kylie, out of prison.

"Thanks babe." He kissed my lips.

"Where's Amari?" I questioned, looking around.

"He's with his mother. They went shopping to get me a gift then they're coming here," he said so smoothly. "I hope it's not a problem that Kari comes. Amari really wanted her to come." Now this nigga know he's reaching. I said I was willing to be cordial and be as supportive as much as I could, but not only did I have a problem with the lying thieving bitch, so did Aubrey. Nasir might've forgot the fuck shit she pulled and how she lied on me, but I didn't.

"Of course that's not a problem, especially since Jaxson and his girlfriend was invited by my mother. He never missed a cookout and the boys wanted him to come." I threw out there. Truth was ,Jaxson was going to pick up the boys but the boys didn't want to miss the cook out so my mom just invited him and his girlfriend.

So it would be a win win situation.

"That's cool." He nodded. "Ava do you have a problem with Kari coming because I can leave if you do, I really wanted to be here with you, but I want them here with me too." Nasir asked, looking at me like he was trying to read me. He knew I would have a problem with her coming to my family function, but I was once again put in a situation where I had to bite my tongue. I hated that I was keeping my truth to myself, but I didn't want to come off as selfish or inconsiderate.

"Nasir, I said it was cool. Just keep her on a short lease."

"Happy Father's Day Nasir," My mom said, coming to give him an ice-cold beer.

"Thanks Ms. Dana. Where's Mr. August?" He asked while giving her a hug.

"You know he's over by the grill smoking that damn pot like we don't have kids around." She fussed, rolling her eyes. Nobody could tell my dad anything in his house.

"How yall got him cooking on Father's Day? I thought this day was catered to the men."

"You try and get him off of that grill. August not letting anyone touch his grill. Cooking on Father's Day is a sacrifice he's willing to make." All I could do was laugh because my dad didn't play anybody touching his grill.

"Let me go speak to everybody."

"Fix your face child. What going on now?" My mom asked after Nasir walked off, rubbing the side of my face. I was trying not to let my emotion show but I was really turn off by this little ordeal.

"Nasir done invited his babymama here because she wanted to spend Father's Day with him, too." I admitted.

"Ava, what I tell you about messing with men with children?"

"You said if I couldn't handle a blended family then don't mess with men with children." I understood the say very clearly and it was not like I couldn't deal with having a blended family. The problems come with the crazy babymamas. Kari was too needy for my liking. Granted, the hoe was pregnant and Nasir wanted to be a part of every moment, but I felt like she was using this pregnancy to her advantage. Just a couple of nights ago she had him running out the house because she was craving fucking Chick-fil-A. It was like she was doing everything in her power to draw a wedge in between me and Nasir.

"Okay, so act like you know. Plus, Jaxson coming."

"Yeah, Jaxson is coming but he's bringing his new girlfriend. So it's not the same."

"Girl stops stressing the small shit. You have the man she wants. Don't bring unnecessary drama in your relationship. If you can't deal with the adjustments in his life then leave him alone. Stop wasting his and your time, because that girl is not going anywhere anytime soon my darling."

"I know," I mumbled.

Kari was worse than Sharell's ratchet ass.

"Come on, Kai is on her way and we have to make sure everything is ready for her surprise."

Today was not only the Father's Day cookout, but it was also Kai and Quadir's baby shower as well. With all of the craziness going on with Kai being attacked, the birth of Miracle, Quadir arrest and Kai's divorce, no one really had time to plan anything. Not only were they going through personal issues, but everybody else was going through their own problems too.

"Hey family," Aubrey yelled, making her presence known. She was walking in with Kylie and Rashawn.

"See, get it together or you'll be confused like ya sister. She doesn't know what she wants, but I can tell you right now, if Rashawn stop trying to right his wrongs and literally just co-parent with Aubrey, she would have a whole heart attack. Aubrey love that man and you and I both know she does. Shit, Tristian was a fucking catch but she never gave herself fully to him and that's because her heart will always belong to Rashawn. She's just suborning and like getting her ass kissed," my mom ranted.

"Why yall over here whispering and talking trash?" Aubrey

complained, walking towards us.

"I ain't talking trash straight facts baby. So, when you going to stop being suborning and make your family whole. A man will only try for so long."

"Mom, don't start. I didn't break up my family. He did!" Aubrey rolled her eyes and turned up her lips. She wasn't stunting anything my mom had to say.

"Okay Aubrey, this is the last thing I'm going to say anything about your situation. Nobody saying Rashawn is innocent, shit, your daddy even threatens to kill him if he hurt you or Kylie again. I'm say what's done is done, and you're not that innocent either. Don't forget that you blamed him for the crazy girl shooting up your wedding when you were part of the blame. Don't act like he wasn't trying to be there for you and you pushed him away. Yall both are wrong now. Just know, no man is going to beg and plead for forever."

"So…" I started, changing the subject. I knew Aubrey was going to say something off the wall and we didn't have time for that at a family gathering. Looking at my phone, I seen that Quadir text saying that they were out front. "Kai's here."

"Yay! I can't wait to hold my baby," Aubrey said excited, overlooking what our mom said and I was thankful she did.

"Everybody, Kai is on her way back her," my mom yelled so everybody could get ready to say surprise.

"Are we early? Why isn't there any music playing?" Kai asked, confused everybody could health them talking walking up the driveway.

"Man, I don't know but what I do know is you fucking playing, wearing that short ass dress. I'm going take you in ya old room and fuck the shit out of you."

These freaks. I thought while shaking my head.

"Naw, we may have to sneak away so you can eat my pussy from the back," Kai replied.

"These muthafuckas must be out of their minds if they think any of that shit going down in my house." My dad was fuming, pacing back in forth.

"Shit, you going to mess around and get knocked up again because I'm bussing all up in that puss..."

"Surprise!" Everybody yelled, cutting Quadir's nasty ass off as they walked into the backyard. The look on Kai's face was hilarious as she turned beet red from embarrassment.

"Oh my god!" Kai muttered, covering her face.

"Don't be shy now. Here I am thinking you're my innocent child and you're a little freak." My mom teased, laughing giving Kai a hug.

"What is all of this?" Kai was looking around the backyard. We had half of the yard decorated in Father's Day decoration and the other half was decorated for a baby shower. It looked ghetto but it was the thought that count.

"Baby, with everything going on in your life and everybody else trying to get their life together., we never had time to plan you a baby shower or a welcome home party for my Miracle baby when she got out of the NIC- Unit. So what better time to do it now while everybody's here."

"Aww thanks." Kai smiled. I knew she didn't think nothing of having a shower because Quadir went crazy and brought everything Miracle needed plus more.

The baby shower/ Father's Day cookout was in full swing and everybody was enjoying themselves. Everyone except me. I was sitting next to my parents bar sipping on a drink. Kari hadn't been here no longer than a half n hour and the bitch had done got on my nerves. First, she walked into my family's backyard like she owned the place and didn't even bother to speak to anyone. Second, she brought her shifty eyes mama who looked like she was about to pick pocket everybody. And last but not least, she acted like Nasir couldn't leave her side or she would die.

"Babe, you cool?" Nasir said, wrapping his arm around me and kissing the back of my neck.

"Oh, you finally have some free time?" I barked with a hint of attitude. I was over this whole scene. I wasn't jealousy, I was just over everything. When Jaxson came, his girl wasn't with him. she was meeting here after work. But, he wasn't all up my ass acting like he couldn't get a plate or anything like that. Kari was so far up Nasir's ass that he couldn't even enjoy himself around his family because she was following him like a lost puppy. I thought she had brought her mama here to make sure she had some company but no, her mom was here looking like she was scoping out my parents' house to steal.

"Ava, what's that supposed to mean? I told ya ass if you had a problem then I could have left. You really making this Father's Day real shitty for me," he had the nerve to snapped in a low tone. It was like he was so blind to the things that Kari did, and this was only her pregnancy. It made me wonder what was going to happen when the baby actually got here.

"Aye Quadir," I heard my dad call out, causing my eyes to divert in their direction.

"Wassup Mr. August?"

"Kai ain't come back from in the house. Bring ya ass over here until she come back outside. I'm not fucking with yall today," my dad then stated, causing everybody to laugh. He wasn't playing with Kai and Quadir.

Turning my attention back to Nasir, I told him, "Nothing Nasir, enjoy your Father's Day." With that said, I turned and walked into the house, leaving him standing there looking stupid. I might've been coming off as a bitch, but at this point, I honestly didn't care. It was just best for me to stay away from him the rest of the duration of the cookout.

"Girl, Nasir fucking with a high-class bitch." I heard someone try to whisper in a low tone. I was walking up the steps after coming inside. Now, everybody knew not to go upstairs in my parents' home. If they had to use the bathroom, there was one downstairs.

"So ... Get out of that girl parent's room." Now I was pissed because I knew this was now Kari and her thieving ass momma.

"Girl, you see her mama out there with all that jewelry on. I know she got some more I can pawn. That bitch probably won't even know it's missing."

"What the fuck yall think yall doing?" I was now standing in the hallway. Kari popped her head out the bathroom so fast that she looked like a deer caught in head lights. Her mama who I believed to be a junkie was so busy putting my mama jewelry in her bag. I went charging after her, punching this old trick in her face and all. How you come to a party uninvited and try to steal?

"Ahhhh!" Kari's mama, Kyra, fell to the floor holding her bleeding nose. I bent down and grabbed her purse and started taking my mama jewelry out of it. I didn't even notice Kari behind me until she push me on the floor. Turning around, I kicked her right in the face.

"Bitch!" Kari yelled, trying to get herself together. I wasn't giving her no time. Straddling her, I started to land blows after blow. The was the straw on the camel's back. I must've of black out because the next thing I knew was Quadir pulling me off Kari and half of my family standing in my parents' room.

"What the fuck is going on?" Nasir barked, looking at me with the death stare.

"Ask ya hoe ass babymama and her thieving ass mama! Up here talking shit and trying to steal my mother's jewelry. I don't even know why ya dumb ass invited these hoes when they stole from ya dumb ass." I shouted, not even caring anymore.

"She's lying! We were in the bathroom because I was spotting blood and she started to fight with me on purpose. I guess she wanted me to miscarriage our baby," Kari cried as she wipe the blood off her busted lip. The look on Nasir's face was a conflicted one. What hurt me the most was that fact that he was considering her story the truth.

"I knew that bitch had shifty eyes! Get these bitches out my house. I opened up my home and you heffas want to steal from me," my mom snapped as my father held her back.

"Dana, calm down. It looks like Ava handled everything."

"Nasir, she's lying! We wasn't stealing anything." Slouching over with her hand pressed against her stomach, Kari said, "I feel cramps. We need to get to the hospital."

"Alright. I don't know what happened here, but I apologize for this happening." Nasir said, turning to my parents.

"I just told you what happen.! You seriously not going to take my word." I was beyond angry.

"Ava, she stating she is bleeding and thanks to you she could possibly be having a miscarriage. No, I don't put it pass you. Every since you found out about this pregnancy you been showing ya ass and not being understanding."

"For the simple fact you allowed that bullshit to come out of your mouth, I see where you stand. It's over! I can't do this any-more," I clearly stated! Breaking up with him was something that should have been done.

"Like, you really making this about you? I never thought you would be this inconsiderate about this situation. So, I see your true colors and I can't fuck with someone selfish like you." Nasir said while helping Kari out the bedroom door. Kyra had a smirk on her face but that was soon whipped of when my mother molly whopped her upside her head.

"Ava," Jaxson called out, walking up to me.

"I'm cool Jaxson!" I replied, walking out the room and down-stairs. Grabbing my keys, I headed on home. I needed some peace and quite to deal with what had just happened.

Chapter 21

Kai

Tonight was the night of my divorce party! I was so happy to finally go out with my sisters and friends and just let my hair down. I had so much respect for all of the mothers out there working and being a parent. Lately I've been thinking about leaving my job due to the fact that I could no longer dedicate my time to my boss the way he needed me to.

My top priority was now Miracle and I needed to focus on her.

Quadir's shop was doing well, and he was sure to tell me every time that I didn't have to work. I just loved making my own money. My settlement with the hospital was coming to a close and I was about to have a big payday. When that money came, I planned on starting a business, being my own boss and creating my own work schedule so that I could cater to my child the way I needed.

"Kai, don't go out with ya sisters acting crazy. Don't make me have to pop up on ya ass because you know I will," Quadir warned, pulling me into him and kissing my lips.

"I'm not, baby. It's all about me having fun. I'm so happy that the nonsense and craziness is over."

"Me too. Be safe and if you're too drunk call me. I'll come pick you up."

"I will, babe. What are yall doing tonight?" I was referring to him and Miracle who was already a daddy's girl.

"She going to spend some time with my mom. I have two late appointments. I have to finish up one of my client's sleeve and his girlfriend want to get tatted too."

"Cool. Let me go. I was been supposed to be at the club." I said, looking down at my phone seeing Aubrey calling me for the third time. When Quadir said okay, I told him, "Miracle should be okay. I pumped enough milk to last her the next two days, because the way I'm about to turn up I'm going to be pumping and dumping for the next twenty-four hours."

"Bye Kai." He couldn't do anything but laugh. "Go on ahead because ya big headed sister calling my phone now." He answered the phone and put Aubrey on speaker.

"Fuck you Quadir!" Aubrey shouted over the loud music "Kai, bring ya ass on. Everybody's here!"

"I'm on my way," I said, giving Quadir one last kiss before walking out the door.

Things had truly turned around for me and I hadn't been this happy in a long time. I was truly surprised that I hadn't heard anything from Mikey since the day me and my sisters popped up on his ass. It seemed like I'd ben excommunicated from his family. The only one who kept in contact with me was his Grandma Lucy. But Ms. Lucy had been my girl. We go way back like four flats on a Cadillac.

Ms. Lucy was the only real one too me when everybody decided to keep MJ a secret. But, from what she told me, Mikey still hadn't stepped up to his responsibilities and Trinity was nowhere to be found. I was pretty sure she wasn't ever coming back due to her being wanted for attempted murder. I just felt bad for MJ because he was an innocent person in a bunch of grown people mess.

As soon as I walked into the club, I spotted my sister and friends already in V.I.P turning up. Aubrey and Ava went all out for this little divorce party. They invited everybody from, Meech and Rome's girlfriends, our cousins on down to our hairstylist, Chasity, and the owner of the spa we all went to Reign.

"Here comes the lady of the hour," Ava announced, I could tell she was already tipsy. It was fucked up that her and Nasir was over but I understood exactly where she was coming from that day at the cookout. Kari was a mess and I commended Ava for trying to stick it out as long as she did.

"Hey yall!"

"Congrats!" Reign and Chasity said giving me a hug.

"I want to make a toast," Aubrey said, getting straight to the point as everybody held up their glasses. "I want to say congratulations to my sissy pooh on her divorce. Some may think we're crazy for celebrating this moment in her life, but this past year have been one trying year, and nd no woman should go through what you went through. We're celebrating because now all of the drama and bullshit is finally out of her life. So, let's toast to new beginnings."

"Cash Money taking over for the 99 and 2000," the DJ shouted in his mic right before the intro to Juvenile song '*Back that Azz Up*'. That was our cue to head to the dance floor. I didn't care what year it was, this would always be the ladies anthem to let loose and twerk what her mama gave her.

"Fuck it up Kai!" Ava yelled, egging me on. I was showing my true ass out here. We were truly having fun until I noticed some girl grilling me on the other side of the dance floor with her friends.

"You know them?" Aubrey asked standing next to me. She'd peeked them eyeing me too.

"I think that's the bitch Quadir use to talk too." The more I looked at her, the more familiar she was becoming. This was the same bitch he had at the restaurant with the caked-up makeup.

"Is there a problem?" Ava asked, walking up on her when she realized we were staring down a group of girls.

"Naw, she obviously still in her feelings about Quadir, but that's personal because my man let her know what it was. It's nobody fault if she wanted to be stuck on stupid," I said and then smiled at her, causing her to roll her eyes. I wasn't about to give her the attention she wanted. She was the one butt hurt over a man that didn't want her.

"Ava?" A deep voice came from behind us. Turning around, it was a handsome man walking in our direction.

"Hey... Semaj," Ava greeted the guy with a smile.

"Damn, ma, you looking gorgeous. I'm surprise to see you here."

"We're celebrating my sister's divorce from a fuck boy. It seems like we keep running into each other."

"Maybe because its meant to be," The guy grabbed Ava's hand and then looked her body up and down.

"Yo' Snake?" Some one called out to the guy as he damn near drooled over Ava.

"Snake?" Ava asked, looking at him confusedly.

"Yeah, that's my nickname?" He answered, looking at his friend with the death stare. It was almost as if he didn't want Ava to know that was his nickname.

"He looks like a snake with those dark beady eyes," Aubrey whispered to me and I agreed. I didn't know what it was, but I was getting a bad vibe from him. But, it could've just been me being an overprotective sister. Ava had a thing for falling for people too quick, and the last thing I wanted was for her to get under another man in order to move on from Nasir.

"Well, I don't want to hold you, but how about we get something to eat at the let out." He asked, and I knew Ava was going to say yes.

"Ummm... Sure, let me get ya number and I'll call you when we're about to leave. We can meet up at a restaurant." I stood here watching them exchange numbers and after that, Semaj when on about his way.

"Ava, where you know him from?" Aubrey asked what I was

thinking.

"Girl, remember the time Nasir basically stood me up at the movies? Semaj is the man I went to see the movie with. He's cool and all."

"Don't go out to eat trying to make love connections and shit."

"I'm not, damn! A bitch is just hungry and he offered and I'm accepting a free meal. Plus, I've been in the house all week dwelling on what was my relationship. I just need a night of fun."

"Alright, just make sure you keep on ya location and if you feel uncomfortable call us." I said. I wasn't going to tell Ava what to do because she was a grown ass woman and she was going to do what she wanted anyways.

"Yall know I don't go anywhere without my taser or pepper spray. Plus, when we went to the movies he was a complete sweetheart."

The rest of the night we partied like never before. I didn't even know Aubrey had me all over her Live, but Quadir seen it and was sending me threaten messages about the way I was dancing. Talking about he was about to come up to the club and drag me out and even said something about how these disrespectful niggas were commenting on the video like he was my nigga. All I could do was laugh at his crazy.

"I had so much fun." I said as we were saying our goodbyes after the club.

"Me too, and I'm happy you did but a bitch is hungry. So I'm about to meet Semaj at IHOP," Ava said, giving us a hug as Semaj walked up to us.

"Treat he right." I gave him a warning look.

"That's the plan," he said walking her to her car. As soon as Ava got in her car I text to make sure her location was on.

"Alright sissy. Where are you going?" Aubrey asked.

"I'm going to meet my man at his shop. Miracle is at his mom, so I don't have to rush home." I heard someone suck their teeth from behind me and it was no other than IT the clown looking bitch. But just like in the club, I wasn't giving her the attention she wanted. I knew she was waiting for me to address it so she can say something but I wasn't fighting over a man that was already mine.

"Alright, text me when you get to his shop."

On my way to the shop, all I could think about was how my life had turned out for the better. My divorce hurt me because I truly did love Mikey. I never even thought I could love another man the way I loved him, but I proved myself wrong. Quadir was everything I wanted and needed in a man. Not only did he satisfy me spiritually but he satisfied me sexually as well. I loved the fact that he allowed me to explore my sexual side unlike Mikey.

"We're closed!" I heard Quadir yelled from the back. I had caught the door as his last two clients left. I made my way to his room where all of his equipment was. "I said we're close!" He yelled again. By the time I had got to the back, he was standing up and turning around only to find me standing in the doorway smiling.

"You had fun?"

"Yes, I did. But I missed you the whole time," I admitted. I loved being around him and our daughter. Just being in their presence made my day better. When I'm at work or alone I missed them terribly and that was the main reason I wanted to quit my job.

"Oh yeah. Why didn't you go home?"

"I want a tattoo." I said smiling.

"Kai, you don't like needles. You don't even have any piercings besides the ones in your ears. And your mom got ya ears pierced when you were a baby." He looked at me like I was bluffing, but I wasn't. I'd been wanting this tat for a minute and this was the perfect time.

"I'm serious and I want you to do it."

"What you want?" He asked, now setting up his station again.

"I want ya name, right here," I said, pulling up my dress and pointing to my right ass cheek. I knew I surprised him, but he was feeling my tattoo idea because he couldn't even hide the silly smirk on his face.

"Cool, get ya ass up on my table."

Doing as I was told, I waited patiently for him to get everything in order. I was nervous but I wasn't going to back out.

"Oh, wait!" I shouted as soon as I felt the needle touch my skin.

"Naw, baby girl, I already started. If I stop I'm charging ya ass double for wasting my time," he muttered, causing me to look at him like he was crazy.

"Why are you charging me in the first place," I groan as he laughed.

"I'm not so sit ya cry baby ass still."

After the first five minutes of the tattoo, I got used to the feeling and in some weird odd way, I was starting to get turned on. By the time he was finished, my thong was soak and wet. Quadir took a picture of it and showed it to me. I had to admit, my baby had skills.

"I guess I know it's real. You done got a nigga name tatted" She said admiring his work. he places plastic over top of it.

"What are you doing?" I asked as he started to pull my thong down my legs and off of me.

"When the last time I ran up in you with out Miracle cock blocking ass crying every ten minutes?" All I could was laugh because it seemed as though no matter the time of day as soon as me and Quadir was ready to have sex Miracle would start trying. "Shit, she probably crying right now," he then mumbled, making me laugh.

"Wait, don't we have to pick her up?"

"You already know Mom Dukes not letting me pick her up tonight. Before I came she made sure I packed extra outfits because she was spending the night."

"I'm surprise you allowed her to keep you daughter."

"I mean, I trust her only because she did raise me?" he said, and he was dead serious. All I could do was shake my head. My baby was going to have a hard time making friends and she could just forget about dating.

Quadir tapped me on my ass and I knew that was his way of telling me to toot my ass up. I arched my back and tooted my ass up in the air, giving the perfect view of my freshly waxed kitty. It was two second before I felt his tongue snake in and out of my honey spot.

"Quadir," I moaned his name as he feasted on my juices. What drove me crazy was when he alternated from eating my pussy to my ass. I had to admit when he first did it I was like, *wait a minute nigga.* But a bitch quickly fell into line after he gave me one of the orgasms of my life just off eating the ass like groceries. So now I be all for it.

"Fuck," I heard him moan as my juices poured into his mouth. Picking me up, he made me straddle him while he sat in the chair he was doing my tattoo in in rolling me in front of the mirror in his room.

"Damn Kai." He groaned, biting my shoulder as I slid down his dick, not stopping until I was all the way down. Whining my hips, I was making sure he was hitting my g-spot with each stroke.

"I'm about to cum " I cried out in ecstasy. Placing my legs in the crook of his arms, he slammed me up and down on his dick intensifying both our orgasms. All I could do was submit to him as we both erupted together.

"Damn, that was fast," Quadir admitted, and I could only laugh. It had been a minute so it was to be expected.

"That was only the first nut," I let him know, climbing off him and squatting in front of him. I took him whole into my mouth. Tonight, I was taking advantage of our little break from parenting. I missed getting uninterrupted dick.

"Kai," he moaned, grabbing my hair. I had him right where I wanted him, and now I was about to transform into Supahead. After this nut, I planned on fucking him like a porn star. You know my baby liked it nasty.

Chapter 22

Aubrey

"Daddy Tristian!" Kylie yelled, running up the steps to the house. Seeing Tristian holding his son brought a smile to my face. Tristian was always a good father to Kylie and she wasn't his biological child. He seemed truly happy and content with his life nowadays.

"Hey baby girl, you ready to go to Atlantic City?" Tristian smiled, giving Kylie a hug.

"Yes, I can't wait to get on the beach." Tristian always took Kylie to the beach around this time of year. "Can I hold my brother? I miss his chunky self," she said, standing on her tippy toes to give him a kiss. Tristian lean the baby down so she can plant her kiss on his cheek.

"Sure, go wash your hands," he replied before Kylie darted into his house.

"Wassup Bree?" He smiled, looking at me.

"Nothing much, just trying to get my life together," I admitted. Things at my house were bad and honestly, it was all my fault. Yes, Rashawn did me dirty but lately it seemed as if his efforts were slowly decreasing. It was like we were more of roommates than anything. I didn't know why I'm so surprise being as though I'd been being a total jerk since he moved back in.

"You want to talk about it."

"Tristian, I don't know what I want. Like, when Rashawn first came home and we decided to make our relationship work, things were great. Then we had that dreadful wedding. I honestly felt we both didn't handle the aftermath of the wedding correctly, but at least I was out her fucking other niggas," I vented.

"So, the question is, are you going to forgive him?" Tristian asked a question that everybody wanted to know the answer to.

"I want too but I will always have the bad memories. Like, he really cheated on me with some bitch that was out here selling pussy."

"He didn't know she was out here selling pussy. He's not even that type of nigga. Are you going to allow the bad memories to override your true feelings? I know what he did was fucked up, and trust me, I know for a fact that he will never do it again."

"Easier said than done." I mumbled.

"Listen, I'm telling you from a man perspective. When you think you lost ya girl all of the games and pride get pushed to the side."

"This coming from Mr. Perfect himself."

"I'm not perfect. I almost lost Keisha," he said, shaking his head. This was news to me because to me, they were the perfect couple. Shit, I was a little jealous that she had everything that I once had. But I couldn't give Tristian what he needed and that was to give myself fully to him.

"What did you do?"

"You remember Felicia?"

"Ya hoe ass boss that I told you wanted you?" I asked, rolling my eyes. His boss had been trying her luck with him since we were talking. Come to think about it, we had plenty of arguments about her

"Yeah, me and Keisha was going through some hard times in our relationships. We were fighting over dumb shit. I let Felicia top me off. Long story short, Keisha found out because she went through my phone. Keisha straight up left me, no questions asked. When I say I was hurt... A nigga wasn't eating or sleeping. I was damn near stalking her. When she finally forgave me, I didn't even want to be on no boyfriend girlfriend level. I need her in my life forever. I will never step out of her again. Her leaving damn near killed me. So, look, all I'm trying to say is, I believe he learned his lesson."

"How did you come to that conclusion?" I wanted to know because the last time they had contact was at the New Years Eve party and Rashawn was so drunk and guilty of his own actions that he accused me and Tristian of sleeping together.

"I came to that conclusion when he came to my house and actually apologized for coming at me wrong and accusing me of sleeping with you. We talked and trust me, he learned his lesson."

"I'm back." Kylie said coming back outside.

"Okay, well I'm going to get going." I had to get to work.

"Bye mommy."

"Bree, take the time out and figure out what you want. What really makes you happy and if the good in yall relationship outweighs the bad." Tristian some last minute advise. I was going to take his words into consideration.

After about twenty minutes, I was pulling up to my job ready to start my shift. Walking through the front door, I got a surprise when I saw Morgan waiting out in the common area. Today was Friday and every Friday he usually takes his grandmother out to eat, but their trips stopped after he killed Amber and Rashawn almost killed him. I felt even worse. It was like he was neglecting his grandmother in order to stay away from me.

"Morgan!" I said, walking over to him. I was just so happy to see him that I didn't even notice the woman sitting next to him.

"Aubrey, wassup?" He stood, giving me a hug. I guess we hug for too long because I heard someone clearing their throat. "Oh, Aubrey, this is my fiancée, Kelly."

"Hello, Aubrey." Kelly gave me a fake smile and extending her left hand, making sure I got all views and angles of the rock sitting nicely on her ring finger.

"Fiancée? Well, I guess congratulations are in order." I was caught off guard and honestly, a little hurt. I wasn't in love with Morgan or anything like that, but I was now having thoughts running through my head about him playing the whole time we were talking.

"Thank you." They replied together in unison. "Kelly, wait here for my grandma. I need to speak with Aubrey real fast."

"Sure. Nice meeting you Aubrey. Morgan make sure you get her information so we can invite her to the wedding." I gave her a fake smile in return and followed Morgan. We walked back outside to the front of my job.

"Fiancée Morgan, really? When did this happen? Just a couple months ago you were single and dating."

"Aubrey, it's not what you think. I never played you."

"Well how are you engage and is this Kelly your ex?"

"Yeah... Listen, the night everything went down at your house made me think about a lot of things. One, it's obvious you had too much shit going on with you. Shit, our second date I killed a psycho bitch and got my ass beat by your deranged ex."

"Morgan.."

"Naw, what I'm really trying to say is that night opened my eyes to my own situation. Me and Kelly's break up was my fault and it took me not knowing if I was about to die or not to know that she was the only girl I wanted to be with. Yeah, it may sound cliché but it's the truth. I never fought for my relationship with Kelly. I just let her out of my life. When I was recovering, she was the only one who had my back. She was the one helped me with my grandmother when I couldn't. I didn't want to come here, and my grandmother see my jaw wired shut and I couldn't explain anything to her. Kelly helped me when I least expected her too, and I can't even begin to explain how much I love her."

"I understand and I happy yall worked things out. I'm happy

that you're happy." I said, and I genuinely meant it. Morgan was a great person.

"So how are you? Did you make things work with ya ex"?

"It's complicated."

"Stop being stubbornning. I'm pretty sure he learned his lesson. Aubrey that man came as soon as he heard ya voice on that girl phone. He loves you and you know it. Don't let your pride let you be lonely. Its only so much a person going to do before they give up. Things can't work if its one-sided," Morgan said then giving me a hug. Pulling back, I swore I seen Rashawn's car pulling out of my job's parking lot.

"Hello, Aubrey," Morgan's grandmother, Mrs. Jones, spoke.

"Hello, Mrs. Jones. Nice meeting you, Kelly. Enjoy the rest of your days." I said giving Morgan one last hug.

Today at work was dragged, maybe because I had a lot on my mind. I was ready for things to get back to normal. I missed Rashawn in more than one way. With Kylie going to the beach for the weekend, maybe me and Rashawn could really work on us. I wanted my family back. It seemed like everybody was finding happiness and I was on team miserable. Everything Morgan and Tristian said was true, and I no longer wanted to be the one in my own way of my happiness. I know Rashawn was beyond fed up with my antics.

Tonight was going to be the night that things got back to normal. After work, I went to the market to make Rashawn's favorite dinner. When I reached my house, his car was not parked outside.

"Let me get in the shower before I cook this food," I muttered to myself. Something was off as I looked around. All of Rashawn's clothes and shoes were gone. He even took the damn Xbox. Calling his phone, it kept going straight to voicemail. All I could think of was my mother's words and they seemed to rang true.

No man is going to beg and kiss your ass forever.

"Fuck, I lost him." I couldn't even lie, I was hurt and heartbroken as the tear started to run down my face.

Chapter 23

Quadir

Ever since Kai had come home with the signed divorce papers from Mikey, everything in our life had turned around for the better. I didn't even know how she got Mikey to sign those damn papers, but she did, and I wasn't going to question her about it. The deed was done. Not only had our relationship been in a good space, our baby, Miracle, was healthy and such an active baby. Kai was currently about to become a business owner. She'd recently settled with the hospital for a couple of million dollars for her and Miracle.

Miracle's money was in a savings account that no one could touch except for her when she turned twenty-one.

Kai was putting good use to her money. She started a children boutique that sold clothing and shoes, starting with preemie sizes all the way up to preteen clothing. She'd finally given up her job working with the lawyer, but he could only compromise so much with her schedule. So, she decided to resign, and she trained his next assistant to do the job just like her before she left. With her owning her own business it allowed her to set her own schedule. I was ready to move forward with our relationship.

It was only right that I give her my last name now that she'd had my baby.

This weekend was the first weekend in a long time that we had just to ourselves. I'd been planning this night for quite some time. As much as I enjoyed my baby girl and taking her everywhere with us, I knew Kai needed some catering of her own. I decided to take her to Miami for the weekend.

We've been enjoying ourselves since we landed on Friday. To-night was Sunday and we were leaving tomorrow morning. Today was all about her and I let her spend the day in the spa getting the works as I planned for our special dinner.

"Look at this," Kai said, looking around in amazement. For our last night, I decided to have a candle light dinner on a yacht.

"You like?"

"I love it, babe, thank you so much. Thank you for just giving me a quick little vacation, but, I'm ready to get home. I miss Miracle."

"I know. I miss my princess too. You are looking good ma," I said taking in her appearance. She had on a white fitted dress that showed all of her curves with plunging neckline with some gold stilettoes.

"Can I get you any drinks?" Our waiter asked as we set down.

"Yeah champagne." I answered. "Did you enjoy your time at the spa?"

"Yes, you don't know how much I needed that," she smiled, grabbing my hand.

"I ordered our food already. We're having steak."

As dinner was serve we talked about our life and what plans we had in the future. I didn't know why I was so nervous at this moment. The waiter was about to bring out dessert and Kai's cherry cheesecake had her engagement ring on top. We'd talked about marriage plenty of times but it wasn't something that she was rushing to happen. I figured that was because her divorce had only been finalized for only a couple months now. However, I knew she never planned to have a child out of marriage. Kai was old fashion and she wanted to have the same last name as her child. I think she always put the marriage conversation on the backburner due to her not wanting to push me into something.

"Yes, dessert! I've been craving a good cherry cheesecake," Kai smile in anticipation to taste her cake.

"Kai," I started, taking her hand into mine. Not only was I praying her answer would be a yes to my question, I was doing this on Facebook live so our parents and family could see her reaction. Our waiter had my phone recording the whole scene.

"Yes?"

"You know I love you, right? I mean, I never thought the day I moved into my house I would find the love of my life. Kai, you've changed me in ways I never thought was possible. I was a man who never took a female serious but you came into my life and made me want to give you everything life could offer you. I believe god put us in each other's life for a reason. You taught me how to love and I was ya reason to let go and love again. Now look at us. We have a beautiful daughter. The only thing left to complete our family is to give you my last name. Will you marry me?" Another waiter came out with the plate of her cheesecake and just like I planned, the ring was on top. She let out an excited squeal looking at the princess diamond cut engagement ring.

"Yessss baby... oh my god." She started crying tears of joy. Grabbing the ring, I placed it on her ring finger.

"Congratulations!" The staff on the yacht yelled bringing out more champagne. Kai asked one of them to take picture of us to capture this moment.

"I think yall going to go viral. Look at all the viewers you have," the waiter said giving me back my phone. Our phone was blowing up from notification saying congratulations. I even got a text from Kayla and Robin saying they better be invited to the wedding. It was a comment on my post from some random females I'd never seen before with a whole bunch of angry face emoji's. I didn't even have to come for the broad because everybody was coming for her hating ass.

"Quadir, you don't even know how happy I am that God placed you in my life. I can't wait to be called, Mrs. Muhammad." Kai whispered into my ear. The rest of the night we enjoyed our stay on the boat and each other's company.

∞∞∞∞

"**C**ongratulation, boss man!" My whole team at the shop scream when I walked into my shop.

"Thanks!"

"Man, you got my lady looking at me asking for her engagement ring. She's talking about Quadir didn't have to wait six years to pop the question," George expressed, shaking his head. All I could do was laugh because I'd gotten a couple of text messages and DMs of my friends cussing me out because their girls had been pressing them about marriage.

"Tell Shelly to chill out."

"Hey everybody," Kai greeted, walking into the door with Miracle in her arms. "Babe, you forgot your lunch."

"Now I see why you marrying her. Shit, in all of the years I'd been with Shelly's bigheaded ass, she never brought me my lunch, and she want to know why she doesn't have a ring. Shit, a nigga hungry, that's why!" George fussed, causing everybody to laugh.

"Well, I actually brought enough lunch for the whole shop," Kai said as Angie's Soul Food catering team came in and started to set up the food Kai brought. "And, I'm happy everybody is here because I have a surprise for you." She then smiled. I didn't know what Kai had up her sleeve.

"So, babe, I'm so happy that you asked me to become your wife. However, this surprise I had planned way before you popped the big question. When I was shot you know I was loaded with medical bills. I was stressed out on how I was going to pay everything, and you spent all of the money you had for the down payment to open your second shop. No matter how much I asked you not too, you spent your hard own money without a second thought. So, I stand in front of you today giving you the deed to your new tattoo shop on South Street." As the words left Kai's mouth, she handed me the paperwork.

Everything was in my name. Baby girl had seriously blown my mind with this. I never expected for her to pay me back for her doctor bills.

"Kai…" I was lost for words. I pulled her into me and gave her a kiss along with my daughter. I truly prayed to god everyday thanking him for putting her in my life, and it was taking everything in me to not shed real tears at the moment.

After we ate, I shut down the shop and everybody was about to drive down to the shop on South Street to check it out.

"Come, babe," Kai called out to me.

"I'm coming. Start putting Miracle into the car," I responded, making sure everything was turned off in the back.

"We're close!" I heard Kai say to whomever had just walked into the shop.

"Oh, you must be his fiancée?" That voice had me seeing red. I'd told Rhonda to stay away from my girl and me. Now this hoe had the audacity to show her face at my shop after I almost killed her dumb ass the last time.

"What the fuck is you doing here?" My voice boomed around the room, causing both Kai and Rhonda to jump.

"So, this is the infamous Kai," Rhonda asked with her nose turned up, looking Kai up and down. I could tell Kai was trying to stay as calm as possible, probably because she was holding Miracle. "How could you ask her to marry you?" Rhonda was driving crazy. She was now in a fit of tears, and I didn't understand why. I'd never even treated this girl more that was.

"I'm going to get in the car. Quadir, handle this girl. Let this be the last time you think it's okay to show your face at his shop or speak to any one of us," Kai warned before making her way to the door.

"Bitch…" Rhonda screamed and went to swing at Kai. Kai turned around to shield our child. I gripped Rhonda up before her fist had a chance to connect. Grabbing her by her head, I snapped her neck, killing her on the spot. I never wanted to commit a murder in front of Kai, especially not in front of Miracle. However, Rhonda trying to fight Kai with my child in her arms was an automatic death sentence in my eyes.

"Quadir," Kai muttered, looking at a dead Rhonda on the shop's floor. I ignored her and called Majesty to send his clean up people to my shop to get rid of Rhonda's body. "She's dead?"

"Yeah," I answered, watching Kai come to terms of what just happened.

"But, you killed her." I could see in Kai's eyes that she was in disbelief by my actions.

"She committed suicide when she thought it was okay to swing on you. Period. And, to add insult to injury, she didn't care that you had my child in your arms," I explained, looking her into her eyes.

"Who are you?" Kai let out a nervous chuckle. "You're out here breaking people's neck and calling a clean-up crew to come pick up the body."

"I'm your soon to be husband!" I knew she was probably fucked up about what'd just happen, but she would surely get over it. When it came to my girls, I was a fucking savage.

Chapter 24

Rashawn

Aubrey had been blowing up my phone every since she realized I had moved out of her house that I bought her. Seeing her in Morgan's face had me seeing red, but I wasn't about to kill a nigga over a female that clearly didn't want to be kept. Obviously, she wanted to move on and I decided it was time for me to do the same. My only focus at this point was Kylie and stacking my money. Just yesterday I dropped Kylie off at home and Aubrey invited me in, standing in nothing but a silk robe.

I knew what she was trying to do but I was over Aubrey and her petty little girl games. I straight rejected her and made my way back out of her front door. Today, I was meeting with my realtor, Christian, to find me a nice two-bedroom condo to move into. Currently I was staying at Rita's, and she was surely reminding me of why I had moved out of her house as a teenager.

"Good morning," Christian's fine ass walked up to me as soon as she hopped out of her car. I wasn't going to lie; baby girl was bad as shit and I wouldn't have mind sliding up in her. However, at this point and time in my life, I didn't need another bitch going crazy borderline phsyco over my stroke game.

"Good morning." I smiled back as my eyes roamed over her body. She was dressed in a tight skirt and blouse, showing all of her curves.

"So, Mr. Rogers, I have a couple of properties to show you in this building that I think you will like."

"Cool, let's get started," I said, following her lead. The first two condos she showed me, which was on the lower level was okay, but it wasn't good enough for me.

"I'm a little disappointed that you weren't interested in the first two condos, but I know for sure you won't be able to say no to this one. Matter of fact, I bet you would want to place your offer in today after seeing it." She spoke with so much confidence.

"We'll see." We headed up to the 29th floor, which was the highest floor in the building.

"This is what we consider the penthouse condo. It's huge and will give you and your daughter enough room to enjoy and spend time with each other. Also, you have enough room for the both of you to go your separate ways. I know we were looking for two bedrooms, but this condo has three. I know most parents use the third bedroom as a playroom for the children. It's totally up to you, though."

"Yeah, I like the sound of that," I said before the door open and slammed shut.

"Rashawn, so you back to this bullshit again?" Aubrey yelled, walking through the condo. If I weren't so irritated with her presence I would've laughed. Babymama came here ready for war, dressed in a all black sweat suit with the matching Tims.

"Excuse me, but this is a private showing. You cannot be in here." Christian said with a lot of attitude making her way towards Aubrey.

"Bitch, try me if you want! Private showing my ass! Rashawn lets go and stop playing! I get your point, now."

"Do you know her?" Christian asked and if I wasn't mistaken I could hear a hint of disappointment.

"Yes, he knows me! I'm his child's mother and his fiancé once he realize I'm done with my childish antics and using the blame game."

"Christian, give us a minute," I demanded, and she walked out of the condo. "Aubrey, what are you doing coming in here like you ready to fight."

"I am! Can't you tell I'm fighting for you?"

"Aubrey, why you want me now? When I was fighting for you, you gave me your ass to kiss. Then I come to your job with flowers, trying to surprise you with, and you smiling all up in Morgan's face. The same nigga I told you to stay away from."

"Baby, what you seen was a final goodbye. I haven't spoken to Morgan since the whole Amber thing. The only reason I seen him that day was because he was visiting his grandma at the nursing home. I don't want him. I want you. Plus, he's engaged to get married."

"So, you think I'm ya back up nigga?" She didn't even know how offended she had just made me.

"No! I want you and only you! The day you must've saw me talking to Morgan I had just ran into him and his fiancée. After you almost killed him, he came to realization that he didn't fight hard enough for his ex. He just let her walk out of his life. When I got home, I was planning to let you know I was done with the foolishness and ready to get back like we were, but you already had your things moved out." I heard everything that Aubrey was saying but it honestly didn't mean shit to me if she couldn't let go of our past.

Our past was rocky and far from perfect.

"Do you seriously want to move forward? I don't want to make steps to move forward and you constantly bringing up the past. I'm not saying you should forget it, though. Our past is something that I think we both can learn from. However, I'm not trying to dwell on it either. If we are moving forward we moving forward with a clean slate."

"We are. Babe, please just give us another chance." Aubrey leaned up on her tippy toes and place a passionate kiss on my lips. Just the softness of her lips had my mans on brick. It had been a minute since me and her shared any type of intimacy.

"I miss you," I muttered in between kissing her neck and leaving my marks on her.

Aubrey pulled away and lowered herself in front of me, unbuckling my belt and pants and pulling them down far enough to pull my dick out.

"I miss you," her freaky ass spoke directly to my dick before she placed him in her mouth and started bobbing her head nice and slow.

"Fuck!" I moaned as I felt myself sliding deeper and deeper down her throat.

The feeling she was giving a nigga had me on cloud nine, especially when she took her right-hand and glide it up and down my shaft with great symmetry, as she sucked my dick. Then, she alternated in between sucking my dick and balls. Aubrey was pulling out her best moves. Had my toes curling in my damn Jordan's and everything.

"Get up!" I demanded because I wasn't ready to bust yet. She did as she was told and started to get undressed. Leaning her over the back of the sofa, I propped her right leg up giving me perfect access to her honey spot.

"Rashawn," Aubrey moaned as I began to stroke her from behind.

"What are yall doing?" Christian yelled, walking back into the condo and saw me and Aubrey going at it like two lost lovers.

"Bitch, get out!" We both yelled like we were in the right. But me and babymama was making up for lost time.

"Aaarrgghh, yall have to get out soon!" Christian stated, turning to leave back out of the condo. I knew she was mad because her face was as red as a tomato.

"I love you Rashawn," Aubrey stressed, laughing,

"I love you too, Aubrey." I replied back to her as I continued our quickie. Christian was right, I was placing an offer today. New beginnings. I needed a new place. Nothing to be reminded of the past, and the house Aubrey stayed in was filled with nothing but bad memories.

Chapter 25

Kari

"**S**nake!" I yelled through the phone. I was currently six months pregnant and too late in my pregnancy to get an abortion. Trust, I asked my doctor for any options and this bitch said adoption. If all of a sudden I decided to go the adoption route, I would be dead on site. It would just prove that I was unfit and Nasir was not the baby father. Snake had been dragging his feet with the plan to kidnap and sell Ava. I gave him all of the information that he needed so I didn't understand what was taking so long for him to put the plan into motion.

"Who the fuck is you yelling at?" He barked back, making me quickly rethink my approached. It wasn't nothing for Snake to hand out an ass whopping, and I knew that.

"I didn't mean to yell." I said, changing the tone of my voice. "It's just, things are taking too long. I gave you all of the information on Ava and her whereabouts. You had plenty of opportunities to get her. What's the holdup? I'm sitting here pregnant with a baby that I'm pinning on Nasir."

"Nobody told your dumb ass to do that shit. I can't just kidnap the girl. It's a process." I looked at the phone like he was speaking a foreign language. Snake must've forgotten he taught me everything about the game. It never took him more than a week to kidnap and sale anyone. If I weren't mistaken, I'd think he'd caught feelings for the bitch.

"Snake, are you trying to back out of this plan? I know you've been wining and dining her. When was that ever part of the plan? Do you like her?" I didn't know why, but I felt a tinge of jealousy.

At one point in time, I did have feelings for Snake but right now, I think my jealousy came from the fact that Ava had every nigga that come in her path nose wide open.

Ever since the Father's Day cookout her family hosted, Nasir had been acting real funny. It was like he was more supportive when they were together. I can admit I was drawling throughout my pregnancy craving and demanding all of Nasir attention, but that was only to get under Ava's skin. I didn't think the dumb hoe was really going to break up with him. Now he's over at his place moping around looking like he lost his best friend.

"Kari, remember, you're the reason why you're in this predicament. Don't question the way I move. Just be happy I'm not going back on my word and kidnap your bitch ass son. You know Ava a good woman, and I wouldn't mind wifing her up." Snake let a chuckle, confirming that he was feeling Ava.

"Snake, think about the money you'll get with selling her. Use your brain and not your dick!" I reminded him. One thing about Snake, he had always been about his money.

"Kari, I got this. I'll let you know when it happens, so you can get ghost. You and I both know ya babydaddy is going to want a DNA test once you have that baby," he said before hanging up without giving me a response.

"What did he say?" Kyra asked, walking out of my bedroom smoking a cigarette and followed by one of her Johns. Yes, my mom was still out here selling ass. I tried to get her to stop because Snake didn't really care. He'd been taking all of the money that Nasir gives me. However, she still out here tricking because she has a nasty drug habit that she can't seem to kick. Every day I look at my mom, I felt like shit. It's like I came back to Philly and ruined everybody life.

"Nothing that I want to hear, and mom, you don't have sell pussy anymore." I was frustrated that things had come to this point.

"Kari, shut the fuck up with your fake righteous ass. Are you going to give me money to buy my percs, codeine, or ecstasy?" She asked, looking at me with a dumb expression on her face.

"No," I mumbled. I didn't even have any money, but if I did I wouldn't help her supply her drug habit.

"Exactly, hoe! You were just doing the same shit I was a couple of months ago. So you can keep your judgement. Now, you on the other hand have other problems. You know everybody in Nasir ear about that baby you're carrying. He's going to want proof if the baby is his. If you can't provide that proof which we all know that baby is truly not his, there's no stopping his derange cousin from killing you. That's if he doesn't kill you first." Kyra said, spitting nothing but straight facts. I could tell by the looks and stares at the cookout that his family didn't believe this was his baby.

"I'm six months pregnant. How can I get rid of this baby?" I asked. Maybe she knew something that I didn't.

"Oh, I have some ways. Let me get dress." She then walked away to the bathroom to shower.

My life was spiraling out of control and I didn't know what to do. I went into the kitchen and found my bottle of Grey Goose and poured me a straight shot. I needed something to take the edge off. Maybe I should've just tried to get ghost on everybody. That would've been a good thing to do, but I knew Snake and he had one of his men following my every move. I wouldn't make it pass state lines.

I was taking shots after shots, and by time Kyra came out of the bathroom fully dressed, in one of my outfits, I was on shot number ten.

"Damn, bitch! What you trying to do, kill the baby with alcohol poisoning?" Kyra laughed.

"No, I just needed to chill before I picked up Amari from daycare. My nerves been crazy lately. I just have a feeling things are going to come tumbling down with everybody pointing a finger at me." It was true. I knew my downfall was near, especially if

Snake didn't do what he had to do. "Come on, its about that time to pick up Amari. I can't be late. You know Nasir is at the tattoo convention in New York with Quadir."

"Oh yeah, come on." Kyra said, grabbing my car keys. Walking out my apartment, I locked my door. "Lets take the stairs."

"Why?" I lived on the fourth floor. Those four flights of steps were hell, so she was out her fucking mind.

"Because the elevator is broken. Saw the sign on there earlier."

Fuck! I had forgotten all about her telling me that earlier today. That's how much I had been in the house. Walking towards the steps, I was swaying due to the alcohol. I held on to the railing to keep my balance.

"Kari, this is the only way to lose this baby," Kyra said before I felt her foot in the back of my back, kicking me down the steps. I went face first and rolled down twenty steps before I landed on the ground in a halt. My body was in excruciating pain. I felt my stomach cramping up and wet substance running down my leg.

"Shit, Kari, we have to get you to the hospital," Kyra said, pulling out her phone, calling 911.

"We have to get Amari." I muttered through the pain.

"No, the daycare will call somebody on his emergency contact list to get him when you don't show up to pick him up."

"Yes, my name is Kyra and I need an ambulance right away to the Greenfield apartments on Chestnut Street. My pregnant daughter fell down the steps and I think she is losing the baby!"

Chapter 26

Semaj aka Snake

After talking to Kari, I knew I needed to make my move fast. One thing she said was that Ava was worth a lot of money and that was the God honest truth. I placed her picture on a private website where men did bedding for the girls, and she was already at two million dollars. But that wasn't surprising. Ava was a gorgeous girl and her natural green eyes make her look exotic. You be surprise how many rich white men buy girls to be their sex slaves or to fulfill some weird fetish that they had.

"Black, yall ready to make this move?" I asked as I jumped into my Escalade.

"Yeah, let's get to her job," Big Black said in his raspy voice. Big Black and Bone was truly the only niggas I trusted. After Kari robbed my ass blind they were the only two niggas who stayed loyal to me. I've been tracking Ava every move and to be honest I felt a little guilty. Ava was about her shit and she loved her kids. Plus, she was cool and down to earth. I could tell the night I took her out to eat after the club she was just trying to enjoy herself.

It was crazy how people had a way of coming into your life and ruin things. That's why it was taking me so long to get her. For the first time in years, my conscious was bothering me. The whole drive, my mind was somewhere else. I was trying to focus and make this process as easy as possible.

"Yo' ain't that her?" Bone said as we watched Ava jog to her car, hurriedly hopped inside and sped off.

"Follow her, but keep a close distance," I commanded.

I was wondering where she was going in such a hurry, and the route that she was taking wasn't to her house. Another thing that was odd was that when I texted her earlier today and she said she was working until eight, but here it was seven thirty and she was rushing from work. After about fifteen minutes with her driving like a bat out of hell, she pulled in front of her kids' daycare. She barely shut her door before running toward to the front entrance.

"Disconnect her battery," I told Bone. He quickly got out of the car and popped open the hood of Ava's car and went to work.

"It's disconnected." Bone said after ten minutes when he got back inside.

"Cool, now we just wait." I didn't want to make her kids apart of my scheme, but shit happens. I needed to settle before people started taking their bids back. Plus, her sons were not too old as to where people wouldn't want to adopt them. That's another huge marketing. There was a lot of desperate people who wanted to have children but couldn't physically have them or adopt them.

"Here she comes right now," Big Black was the first to notice her. I was now parked up the block. I had the perfect view of her but she couldn't see me. To my surprise, she didn't come out the daycare with her kids, she came out with Kari's little boy which was even better. Kari thought all was forgiven because she helped me with this lick with trafficking Ava, but they didn't call me Snake for nothing. I was a grimey ass nigga that was about to go back on his word.

"Change of plans, we'er kidnapping Ava and selling her, and that little nigga is Kari's son. We're holding him for ransom." Selling Ava was already going to double amount of money that Kari stole from me, but its nothing like settling the score and making some extra coins. I watched Ava place Amari in the car seat before getting in her car and tried to start it multiple times.

"This my cue damsel in distress," I mumbled, pulling out the parking spot and making my way down the street, stopping right in next to Ava.

"Ava?" I asked, hoping out the car.

"Hey Semaj," she said, letting out a frustrated breath. "What are you doing here?"

"I was just riding by and saw your car." I lied as she looked at me with confusion.

"I thought you said you was going to back down to Atlanta?" *Fuck!* I forgot I told her that bullshit lie earlier.

"Oh, yeah, I missed my flight so I'm heading out tomorrow," I replied, and she looked at me skeptical.

"It's funny how you always seem to find me," she then said, shaking her head.

"What's going on with your car?" I quickly changed the subject. I didn't like what she was insinuating. Was I stalking her? Yes, but the bitch was trying to make it seem like I was pressed, and that was one thing I wasn't.

"It's not starting," she mumbled. Looking inside the car, I saw Kari's son Amari grilling me the fuck down like I was talking to his woman.

"My man is a mechanic. How about yall step out?" I suggested.

"Naw, we're good. I have triple A. I'm about to call them now."

"Ava, let me be a gentleman and give yall a ride home." I knew I was being persistent and the way she was looking at me, I knew she was starting to feel uneasy. Out my peripherals, I could see Big Black and Bone walking up. I hated to do this dirty, but Ava wasn't giving in.

"Semaj, I said we're good, thanks but no thanks," she said, and when she went to shut the door, I stopped her and dragged her out the car. She was kicking and screaming. We were the only ones outside and everybody from the daycare had left when she walked out the door with Amari.

"Get the boy!" I demanded. As soon as the words left my

mouth, it seemed like Ava turned into wonder woman. Breaking free from my grasped, she ran around the car and started to attack Big Black as he was trying to get Amari out of the car seat.

"Calm ya little ass down, Ava!" I tried to warn her, pulling her off Big Black. Bone pulled the car up and Big Black hopped in the back seat with the kid.

"HELP!!!!!!!" Ava screamed as I pulled her towards my car. I could hear people's doors opening. So, I had no other choice but to punch her in the face, knocking her out cold.

Chapter 27

Nasir

I was finally on my way back to the city of brotherly love from the big apple. I was coming home after supporting Quadir and his crew in the New York annual tattoo convention. I needed this weekend to myself. Things had been hectic lately, ever since me and Ava had the big public breakup in front of our family. Yeah, I regretted my part in the downfall of our relationship, especially now since I was having major doubts about Kari's unborn child. I hated to admit it but Quadir and Rashawn was right. I invested too much of my emotions and money to this unborn child who may not even be mine.

Kari had been moving real funny. Just last week I had to force her to go to her damn doctor's appointment. Seeing her so careless when it came to the care of her unborn child had me wondering why she kept the damn baby in the first place. I knew deep down it was probably because Rashawn wanted her head on a silver platter. She knew the only reason why he didn't touch a hair on her head was out of the love and respect he had for me.

I never meant to blow up at Ava the way that I did, but it was frustrating that every time Kari needed me it was always an issue with her. When Kari came to me stating that she was bleeding, I expected Ava to be more understanding, not start an argument. I just truly regretted the whole situation because when I took Kari to the hospital they stated it was nothing wrong with her or the baby. They couldn't even tell she was bleeding. They just kept her overnight for observation.

As much I didn't want to admit it, I had a gut feeling that Kari had been playing my ass all along, especially when it came to my relationship with Ava. It was like now that Ava and me were over, she had no interest of being a mother.

"Damn, who blowing up your damn phone?" Quadir questioned as we were just passing the *Welcome to Pennsylvania* sign.

"I don't know this phone number," I mumbled. It was the fifth time they had called me. I kept ignoring it because I didn't answer calls that I didn't know, but being that they seem persistent, I went on and answered this one time. "Who dis?"

"About fucking time you answered your damn phone? I've been call you all damn day." The person on the other line screamed into the phone.

A scowl plastered on my face. "Who the fuck is this?"

"Kyra.... Kari's mother! How don't you know my number? And watch your mouth talking to me like that."

"Yo' what do you want?" She'd clearly just pissed me the hell off.

"I was calling to let you know that me and Kari is currently at the hospital right now. She fell and had a miscarriage yesterday. Meet us at Jefferson hospital," Kyra said before hanging up.

To be honest, I didn't know if I wanted to jump for joy or mourn. The only reason why I would be mourning was because Amari was looking forward to becoming a big brother. I truly felt like this was a blessing in disguised. I already had my lawyer on standby to serve Kari with custody papers of the baby came back mine. I tried to be understanding and supportive but it seemed as though Kari was not meant to be a mother.

"What's going on?" Quadir asked once my call had ended.

"Kari had a miscarriage," I heard Quadir grunt under his breath. Ever since Kari opened her mouth saying that she was pregnant, all of my family had their doubts. It was just so convenient that she popped up saying she was pregnant after she pulled that extortion shit with Rashawn. "You don't even have to say shit."

"Sorry for your loss, if the baby was yours. What hospital they're in?" I knew my brother and he wasn't really sorry. It was just the polite thing to say.

"They're at Jefferson," I murmured and Quadir started driving in the direction of the hospital.

After twenty minutes of driving, Quadir and me were standing in front of Kari's hospital door. I could hear the TV on and Kari crying with Kyra fussing at her.

"Kari, this was something that had to happen," Kyra hissed as I walked into the door.

"Mom..." Kari's words were cut short as she noticed Quadir and me standing in the room.

"What had to happen?" Quadir asked before the words could leave my mouth.

"Nothing! She's just really upset because the baby died. I'm trying to let her know God gives his toughest battles to his strongest soldiers," Kyra said, trying to sound religious. The look on Kari's face was more of anger than sadness.

"Kari, are you okay?" I asked, even though I was having my doubts, there was no reason for me to mean.

"Yes. I'm just really fucked up about this. I know how much you and Amari were looking forward to this new baby." She sobbed.

"How did ya dumb ass fall down the steps?" Quadir asked, unbothered by her crying. I swear this nigga was the rudest muthafucka I had met, but his question was a valid one.

"Hello, Kari, how are you feeling?" A nurse walked in.

"Fine giving..." she said looking around the room as to say she was okay sense she was in the hospital, but the look the nurse gave her was one of annoyance.

"Watch them eyes little girl," Kyra snapped, rolling her eyes at the nurse like a five-year-old child.

"Are you family?" The nurse looked at my brother and me and asked.

"I was the baby's father," I answer and I heard Quadir mumbling in the back of me.

"Okay, well, I was coming in let you guys know of some support groups. This will be a hard time for the both of you and support groups are some of the best ways to learn how to move forward," I nodded, and she handed me the pamphlets. Looking through the pamphlets there was plenty of different support groups, one that helped you understand miscarriages and the copping with the lost of a child. The pamphlet that caught my attention was AA (alcoholics anonymous).

"Why is there an AA pamphlet in here? Was she drunk? Was that the reason why she fell down the steps?" I asked the nurse who gave me a look of sympathy. As for Kyra and Kari, they looked as though they were ready to shit bricks.

"I'm not at liberty to discuss due to the patient confidentiality. Kari, you will be being discharge soon." The nurse said before walking out of the room.

"Listen Nasir..." Kari started but I didn't want to hear any excuses she was about to throw at me. I couldn't wait to get home and tell my lawyer to serve her with these custody papers for Amari.

"Where's Amari?" It was a Saturday afternoon and my mother didn't say she picked him up. Kari and her mother both looked stuck on stupid and they looked at one another.

"What? Yall bitches don't hear him asking yall a question?" Quadir's voice boomed throughout Kari's hospital room. I could tell his patience was running thin with them. As for me, I was becoming worry and their silence was pissing me of.

"I don't know," Kari finally answered in just above a whisper.

"What the fuck did you say?" I moved so fast across the room and gripped her up by the hospital gown she was wearing.

"Nasir let her go!" Kyra shouted and I could hear the fear in her voice.

"Nasir, I'm sorry. I passed out after I fell down the steps," Kari sobbed.

"Ya dumb ass didn't think it was a smart idea to pick up your grandson from the school?" Quadir hissed through gritted teeth.

"I.... I... was trying to be here for my daughter." Kyra tried to justify her actions. "I'm pretty sure they called someone on his emergency contact list."

"Get dressed," I demanded Kari to do.

"She wasn't discharge yet." Kyra snapped.

"Bitch, if you don't shut up I'm going to stab you in the side of your fucking neck with my damn hunting knife," Quadir warned, pulling his knife out and placed it to the side of her neck. Kyra had the most terrifying look on her face.

Kari did as she was told, and I started to make phone calls. Just like I knew, my mother didn't have Amari and Quadir and Ava was the only two other emergency contacts on his paperwork, and Ava wasn't answering her phone. Calling the daycare director, she told me that Ava was the one that had did picked Amari up.

"Call Kai and see if they spoken to Ava." As soon as Kari was dressed, we walked out of the room and the hospital. Even though Ava and me wasn't on the best of terms, I knew she would have reached out to me, or someone, to let me know she had my child. This whole a situation was out of character for Ava and now I was really starting to get worried, and not just for Amari's safety.

"Naw Kai said nobody have heard from her, and her kid's dad have her kids. Everybody been trying to reach her since yesterday."

"I'm driving by the daycare," I muttered to myself and basically broke every traffic laws to get there. Pulling up, I saw Ava's car sitting out front and it looked ram shack through. The keys were still in the ignition and that was a bad sign. Now I had a feeling that someone had taken her and my son, but Ava was a well-liked person and I didn't know of her to have enemies.

What the fuck?

The ringing of my phone broke my thoughts. Getting back into the car, my phone connected to the Bluetooth. "Yo' who this?" I snapped in irritation.

"I'm the nigga that has your bitch and son!" The voice said and then started laughing. I could hear Amari in the background crying. I swear my breath got caught in my chest. Who the fuck would come after my girl and child? Looking around the daycare, Quadir looked pissed. Kyra and Kari had a look of nervousness and Kyra was crying so much that she was making herself sick.

"What the fuck do you want? You better not touch them or I'm going to kill you with my bare hands." I was fuming.

"See, lets not throw out bullshit threats. That will only make me do some fuck up shit just to prove a point. Ava's such a beautiful girl."

"Snake, you weren't supposed to kidnap my son!" Kari cried out, causing Quadir and me to snap our necks in her directions.

"Kandi, baby, that's you? I know you didn't think I was actually going to keep my word. Bitch you done stole a quarter of million dollars from me." He called Kari by some name I didn't even know she went by.

"Naw, I need my money, and ya babydad the one who's going to give it to me. If not, Ava will be on the next cargo ship to the highest bidder. You know, people are offering two million dollars for her. You were right; she is going to make me a lot of money. Now I feel I need to triple my profit if you want your son back, and match the offer I have for Ava. If you want both of them back, double my offer. I'll give you twenty-four hours to give you the information about the drop." The person I now knew was Snake said.

"How do I know they're okay? Let me speak to Ava or Amari." I was fuming so bad that I turned around and pistol-whipped Kari and she let out a gut-wrenching scream.

"Daddy," Amari's voice came through the car speakers.

"Son, are you okay?"

"No, this man took me and Ava and he hit her. She's hurt daddy." Amari cried, which broke my heart. I couldn't believe I allowed Kari's dumb ass around in order to allow her to let this happen. To think that I went to bat for this bitch. Against my own girl now my girl caught up in some bullshit that had nothing to do with her.

"Babe..." I was trying to stay strong and not cry after hearing their voices.

"Ava, don't worry. I'm coming to get you and my son. Are you okay?"

"No... I'm so sorry," she mumbled. I couldn't understand how she thought this could've been her fault.

"That's enough, they're alive. You just worry about getting my money," the nigga Snake said. I could tell he was trying to snatch the phone from her. All I could hear was tussling before I heard something break.

"He's hurting her!" Amari screamed in the background before the line went dead.

How the fuck was I going to come up with millions of dollars to save my family?

Chapter 28

Ava

Opening my eyes, I automatically started to panic because I didn't feel Amari around me. The last thing I remembered before everything went black was being on the phone with Nasir telling him me and Amari have been kidnap. I was scared out my mind. I knew I felt bad vibes from Semaj or should I say Snake, when his crazy ass started popping up everywhere I was. At first, I thought it was just a coincidence at the movies, the club, now his ass had done popped up at my kids daycare. I'm so happy Noah and Noel wasn't with me. I hated Amari was mixed into this crazy psycho situation.

I promise I was not going down without a fight.

I was so mad at Nasir for keeping utter faith in his bum ass babymama. Like, how many times did a bitch have to show you that she was unfit in order for you to realize that everybody couldn't be trusted around your kids? I didn't care if the hoe was Amari's mother.

I was now mad at myself because deep down, I felt like Snake was stalking me and I didn't notice. Like how else would he know where I keep finding me? Now I have Amari mix in this mess. The only reason I went to go pick Amari up was because Kari didn't pick him up. They tried to call Nasir and Nasir's mother, and I was honesty the only other emergency contact that could possible get him because Quadir. Kari was straight up ignoring the daycare's calls that the director was about to call the police for abandonment. So it was a good thing I'd answered my phone when I did.

"Amari!" I screamed, trying to stand up but Semaj had my hands chained to the bedpost of an old bed.

"Ava," I heard her cry out to me. Looking around, I still couldn't see him.

"Get me the fuck out of these chains! Semaj!" I screamed. We were currently in what looked like an abandon house with old furniture.

"What you doing all of this yelling for?" Semaj came walking into the room with Amari who poor self had tears falling from his face. As soon as he saw me, he ran full speed and jumped on the old dirty bed, holding me for dear life.

Please God keep Amari and me safe. I silently prayed. I needed to get us out of this house.

"Look at his little bitch ass. You would think you was his mother and not Kari's hoe ass." Semaj chuckled, lighting up his cigar.

"Don't call him out his name! He's a child and your creepy, probably pedophile ass kidnap him." I snapped. I couldn't understand how Semaj could call him out his name like he wasn't putting Amari and me in a traumatizing situation. "Wait... what did you say? You know Kari?" I asked, knowing I had to have heard him incorrectly.

"Oh, you caught that, huh? Yeah, I know Kari. She's my hoe and owes me a lot of money. The plan was to originally kidnap her son here and have her babydad pay some ransom, but she came up with a better idea that was going to double, maybe triple, my profit with the way the bids are coming in for you."

Bid? What hell is he talking about?

"I see you looking a little confused, so let me enlighten you," he spoke through a crooked smile, blowing the smoke from the cigar in my face. "I'm Snake. I'm a muthafucka's worst nightmare. I'm the type of man who would rob a man blind and sale a woman to the highest bidder. I'm the go to guy when the creepy ass white rich men or sadistic men wants to buy their own little sex slave. I'm the king of human trafficking. You my dear is going to make me a lot of money. The bid for you is up to 2.5 million dollars."

All of the sudden, I felt sick to my stomach. I couldn't believe this man had just admitted to having me human trafficked. I'd always heard crazy stories of women and little kids going missing, but I never thought for one second that I would be a victim of it. All I could think about was my sons and probably how I would never see them again.

"I already have a married couple in Maryland trying to buy Amari. You won't believe what people will do to have a kid of their own and they can't adopt."

"If you were just going to sale us to the highest bidder, why did you contact Nasir?"

"I'm a greedy man. One thing I know about men of Nasir caliber, he loves you and love his son which mean he would pay or do anything to get yall back safe and sound. Why not triple my profit and still ruin Kari's life?"

I couldn't hold back my tears after hearing all this, and before I knew it, a fresh set of tears was trickling down my face.

"Ms. Ava, don't cry," Amari said wiping my eyes dry. I tried to stay strong, but my reality was getting to me. I was so mad that my life had turned upside down because some bitch owed some pimp money.

"The sad thing about it Ava, you're truly a beautiful woman. So beautiful that I can't pass up the opportunity to get a taste before I sell you. I always test my product." Snake then put out his cigar than made his way towards me.

"You going to rape me in front of Amari?" I asked with pleading eyes.

"I don't give a fuck if this little nigga sees?" He grabbed my pants and yanked them until they were off.

"Get off her!" Amari jumped up and started to swing his little arms at Snake. To my surprise, he was actually landing some blows, but of course they didn't faze Snake. He simple pushed Amari off the bed and continued to undress me. I could hear Amari's soft cries as he watched with anticipation as to what Snake were going to do next. When I felt him push my legs apart, exposing my privacy.

"Amari, please turn your back and look the other way," I begged Amari, trying to protect him from seeing me get violated.

"Yeah, little nigga, turn the fuck around," Snake ordered before he dived head first and started to eat my pussy like it was his last meal. "Bitch, moan like you're enjoying this," he demanded but I couldn't move or utter a word. How could I pretend to enjoy someone taking advantage of me? After what felt like eternity, he stopped eating me out long enough to pull out his dick. This fool didn't even bother to put on a condom.

"Ahhhh!" Snake screamed as he felt my powerful kick to his nuts. I prayed that I'd just broken his dick. There was no way I was about to allow this man to fuck me. I was going to fight as much as I could, even though my hands were currently chained to the bed. "You bitch!" Snake then barked, punching me in my face. The first punch had put me in a daze, but I continued to kick my legs, landing as many powerful kicks as I could. However, the two-piece that he landed to my face made me quickly give up the fight that I had no chance of winning.

"Please, stop hitting me," I begged. I could feel my lip was busted and swelling. I could taste the blood that was coming from my nose and mouth. I was so defeated that I laid perfectly still waiting for him to have his way with me, and praying to god that it will be over fast.

"I thought you would start seeing things my way," he said. Then he leaned down and spit on my pussy like I was just a hoe in the street. He was trying to get me moist down there because clearly I wasn't going to do it by myself. "Yeah, I feel her getting wet for me," he had the nerve to say right before he rammed his dick inside of me. At this moment, I knew I would never be the same. I felt so defeated and I could hear Amari sobbing, looking directly at me feeling defeated too, as Snake enjoyed the feeling of raping me

"Get the fuck off her!" I heard a gun cock back and it seemed like everything went still, except Snake who was still pumping in and out of me, trying to get his last nut.

Chapter 29

Rashawn

"**M**uthafucka!" Nasir barked as his gun went crashing across Snake's face. Pulling him off of Ava, he then started beating his ass with his bare hands. All you could hear in the room was Nasir's fist and feet connecting to Snake's body, and the sounds of bones cracking.

The sight in front of me would've brought any man down to his knees, and I could only imagine what Nasir was feeling at the moment. Walking in on Snake raping Ava broke my own damn heart. I couldn't wait until I could kill Kari, who was standing in front of me with my gun trained to the back of her head. I could hear her sobbing, which only pissed me off even more. The nigga Snake wasn't as smooth as he thought he also didn't an anybody loyal to him.

His two goons Black and Bone who now had bullet holes between both their eyes had sold him out.

When he called Kari's phone, she broke down and told us how she set up Ava to get sold by Snake so her debt could be paid in full, but what she didn't know was Ava had Amari with her when he went to kidnapped her. Finding out their plan had Nasir on go, ready to fuck up everything walking. He was so messed up and the guilt weighed so heavy on his shoulders from Kari willingly putting Ava in danger just to save her own ass that he wasn't thinking clearly.

We came up with the perfect plan. We got Kyra to call Bone who was one of Snake's goon and told him to come by Kari's apartment. Bone came with his partner and they both thought they was about to run a train on Kyra and Kari. What fucked me up was finding out Kari was out here selling pussy. When they came, they we're greeted with guns in their faces. I saw niggas blinded by pussy so many times. It was sad to say, that was a trap that would always get someone killed.

Within ten minutes of trying to act tough, they both sang like a canary. Maybe it was because Quadir low-key sadistic ass was playing tic-tac-toe on their bare chest with a blowtorch that he kept in his trunk for some odd reason.

"Where the keys for this chain and lock that he has around her arms?" Quadir asked, pushing Kyra in front of me so I could have my gun train on both, her and her bum ass daughter. Looking around with no luck of finding the key, he came back with an axe.

"Ava, I need you to be very still." I could see she was nervous. I was nervous too that this nigga was about to chop her damn hands off. With one swift and precise swing, Quadir cut the chain off of her hands. Covering her up, Amari ran into her arm and sobbed uncontrollably. I knew he was going to be affected by this. Little cousin at the age four witness his dad girlfriend get raped.

"Baby, it's going to be okay. I'm okay," Ava tried to comfort him.

"I tried to save you," he muttered with so much sadness in his voice.

"I know." Ava kissed him on the cheek before Quadir picked him up and allowed her to get dress.

"Nasir, we need to get her to the hospital." I stated because she needed to get checked out.

"No! I don't want anybody to see me like this." Ava shouted.

"Ava...." Nasir said walking up to her with Snakes blood covering his hands. Snake was barely hanging on to life.

"If you don't want to go to the hospital. I'll have the street doctor check you out. You have to get treated for any type of diseases that he could've transmitted to you, and it look like your nose is broken." Quadir voiced, pulling out his phone to make the call.

"Amari, baby, are you okay?" Kari asked her son like she wasn't the reason he was put in this predicament. It was like everything stopped when Ava heard her voice. Without notice, she ran over to Kari and started beating the dog shit out of Kari.

"Please, stop her," Kari begged only for Ava to kick her in the face.

"You trifling ass bitch! Not only did you have this nigga try to sale me to the highest bidder. Did you know he was ready to sale Amari too? He already had a couple willing to pay top dollar for him." Ava screamed in between throwing punches.

"My mom made me do it!" Kari cried out. Obviously she was ready to throw everybody under the bus.

"Bitch.... No I didn't! Nasir, she was lying to you're the whole time about the pregnancy. That wasn't even your baby she was carrying. She been out here selling ass and blowing niggas off to make up the money she stole from Snake." Nasir cocked his gun back and sent a bullet into Kyra's dome without warning, and then turned around and riddled Snake's body with the remainder of bullets.

"Let's go, the doctor is meeting me at your house," Quadir said to Nasir.

"Go head, I'll handle the rest," I stated, referring to Kari. No matter how mad he was, I knew he would never be able to live with himself killing Kari for the simple fact that he would have to look Amari in the eyes everyday.

"Nasir, please don't leave me here with him," Kari begged. Nasir looked at her with so much disgust and she knew him saving her was a lost cause. "Please, just let me say goodbye to my son."

"Naw, I'm not bringing him back in here." Quadir had already put Amari in the car who had Anthony inside.

"Please..." She cried out.

"No!" with that being said, Nasir grabbed Ava's hand and walked out the bedroom door.

"Make this quick!" Quadir demanded, walking out behind them.

"Rashawn, please, I'm sorry. I was just doing what I had to do for the safety of my child."

"You don't have to explain shit to me, because I'm still going to kill you," I chuckled. Pushing her on the same bed that Ava was just chain too, I grabbed one of the zip ties out of my back pocket and tied her to the headboard like Snake had Ava when we walked in this bitch. I also grabbed the belt that was laying on the floor and tied her feet to the bars of the foot board.

"Here," Quadir came back with two cans of gasoline and placed them on the floor and left back out. What caused me to laugh was the simple fact that Kari had the nerve to be praying to God like I wasn't about to send her to hell with gasoline draws on.

I started to pour the gasoline all over the room and on the bodies of her mother and that nigga Snake. Last, I poured the gasoline on Kari, making sure she was drench. She immediately started coughing and choking.

"Rashawn, can you please tell my son I love him," she asked with tears running down her face.

"Fuck no and stop calling him your son because you were never a mother to the youngin. You wanted to be a mother only when Ava was picking up your slack and was jealous. You're nothing but a conniving evil ass bitch that was okay with selling other women into human trafficking. Naw, just know your son will never have any good memories of you."

Lighting a match, I threw it on her body and it became engulfed in flames. Her screams pierce my ears as I walked out the house without giving her so much of a second look. Hopping in the car I prayed that this was something that Ava and Amari would be able to move on from.

Chapter 30

Mikey

It had been months since my divorce with Kai had been finalized, and I wasn't going to lie, I was hurt to see how things ended with my ex-wife and me. Kai was my everything. Not only was she my wife, at the time, but she was also my best friend, my counsel, and the only person who would have never judged me no matter where I fell short. Kai was my ride or die. Half of the things I had in my possession were only because of her. So, living without Kai was a hard pill to swallow.

It was crazy how one mistake could change your life forever. I really lost my soulmate over one night of pleasure that I could barely remember. Kai was a lost that I was forced to deal with. After everything she had been through, from me and my drama to Trinity and her disrespect she brought to Kai, not to mention her trying to kill her and her unborn child, I felt she deserved the peace and happiness that I couldn't bring her.

I was once fighting for a relationship and bond that I had broken. I pushed her to the point where she didn't want anything to do with me, and truthfully, I couldn't even blame her

Right now, I was at the point in my life where I just wanted to be a good father to MJ. I'd been a total dick and a deadbeat, and was so ashamed by my behavior. I was so blinded by the fact that I was losing my wife that I was willing to accept her unborn and neglect my own child.

Not only did I fail MJ Trinity had been missing in action since the day she'd dropped MJ off on the step of my parents. I'd been calling and texting her phone ever since she hit Kai, trying to check her about that.

At first, I was leaving threatening voicemails and texts messages telling her I was going to kill her, especially if Kai didn't make it. Then my anger grew from her abandoning me with a child she knew I wasn't ready to have or deal with. Now lately after not hearing from her, the only messages I'll leave her is begging to call me back so I can at least know she was alright.

When I found out what Trinity had done, I was broken. Now that I was being completely honest with myself, I'd ruined two women lives because of my own selfishness in a sense. The obvious was how I'd affected Kai's life, but Trinity was a different story. Yes, she trapped me, but I was wrong. I should have never cheated on my wife. Secondly, I should have never led the mother of my child on. In the beginning when I found out about the pregnancy I was angry but happy that I was getting the child I longed for. I was very supportive throughout the pregnancy up until she wanted everybody to know about my son. I agreed to let my family know and everyone was excited, except for Grandma Lucy. Her loyalty to Kai was very strong.

My change of heart came when Trinity wanted me to become public about me being a father. I couldn't do that. I would never willingly hurt my wife. Me having an outside baby would have broken her and it did. At the point and time in my life MJ was something I was willing to lose in order to keep my marriage and wife happy.

I say I ruined Trinity's life because I fed into her fantasy of us becoming a real family. When Kai was in the coma, Trinity took on a role of being my wife. She was doing everything in her power to satisfy me. I took that for granted even when I knew my feelings did not carry as much weight as Trinity. I guess you could say I wanted the best of both worlds.

Kai being in my world meant the most to me. Now I regretted that because Kai and me were now over. She had a family of her own and here I was, picking up the broken pieces in my life, and trying to build a relationship with my son who is about to turn one. I missed almost a whole year of his life chasing after my old life.

I was currently in the process of selling the house Kai and me once shared together. There was nothing but good and bad memories. However, lately it seemed like the bad memories outweighed the good. I didn't want to continue staying in the house that was built for my ex-wife and me, and the kids I prayed we would have someday, when we all knew that would never happen.

I just wanted a family of my own now, and as crazy as it seemed, I truly wanted it with Trinity. Kai and her child were perfectly fine, so I needed to move on with my own little family. I knew what Trinity did to Kai was inexcusable, but she was MJ's mother and I needed her here to help me raise our son. I'd been thinking a lot about what my mother said before Trinity went off the deep end. Too much damage was done to fix my marriage. I should have cut the ties a long time ago and tried to make the family thing work with Trinity.

Now she was missing in action and I didn't know if she was just hiding or something bad had happened to her. I was ready to pack me and MJ things and move from Philly, but the only person that was preventing that from happening was Trinity. I wasn't saying I loved her, I just knew she was the only one who would make my family complete.

"Dada," MJ smiled, clapping his hands, excited to see me. I'd just pulled up to my parent's house. I was at my gym handling some paperwork and only stopped by to pick up my mom and MJ. They were going with me to meet the realtor to hand her my keys. She had an offer to buy the house and wanted to do a viewing. After that, I planned on taking my mom and son out to eat for Sunday brunch.

"Wassup, little man?" I greeted, walking up the front steps to the porch.

"Watch this, Mikey," My mom smiled with excitement, standing MJ up. "Go head and show daddy what you can do."

Nothing could make me happier than seeing my son taking his first steps to me. I knew he would be walking soon because MJ had no problem with running everybody over with his walker. I was such a proud father at the moment that MJ was walking before he was even one.

"Go Man! Go man!" I yelled, and MJ stopped and started dancing to the tune of me saying, go man. I couldn't believe my selfishness made me almost miss the best thing that could have happened to me, which was being a father. Picking MJ up, I playfully threw him in the air and kissed him all over his face when he landed back into my arms.

"That's what I like to see," Grandma Lucy said, smiling. Going through my break up from Kai and my divorce, I changed into a person that no one knew, nor liked. It was crazy because I thought by now Kai's crazy ass boyfriend... I apologize, her fiancée, Quadir, would have been found me for sending him to jail the day Kai had their daughter. That was a bitch move and I even could admit it. My thought process was all fucked up. I felt like if I couldn't be with Kai, he shouldn't either. Thinking back on the day of getting him locked up the day their child was born was underhanded and foul, but I guess Kai kept her word because I hadn't heard or seen him since that day at the hospital.

"Yes, mom. Mikey have matured and grown up. I'm happy of the father he's becoming."

"Me too. I love you grandson." Grandma Lucy smiled, weakly. She told me she loved me all the time, but this time seemed to be different. I prayed she wasn't getting sick again and didn't want to tell anybody.

"What's wrong mom?"

"Nothing, I'm just tired. I've been having dreams that something bad is going to happen to this family. So I'm making sure everybody know I love them." In a weird way, Grandma Lucy's dreams always seem to come true. Like, she was always the first to know when someone's pregnant because she always having dreams of fishes.

"Grandma Lucy, everybody's good. Stop stressing. How about you come with us. We're just dropping a set of keys to the realtor then going to brunch." I didn't even know why I didn't been give the realtor the keys. Everything was already moved out the house except my furniture. I'd been staying at my parents ever since I got myself together.

"Okay."

I grabbed MJ's diaper bag and took him to the car and buckle him in. As soon as my mother and grandmother got in the car, I drove straight to my house to meet the realtor. Pulling on the block, I was confused as to why there was at least seven police cars surrounding my house.

"Yall, stay here! I'm going to see what's going on," I ordered to my mom and grandma who had looks of concern fixed on their faces. The police being here had to have been a big misunderstanding.

"There he is!" I heard Trinity's father yelling and screaming, charging in my direction. "I know he did something to my daughter." By this time, he had the police attention and they were all coming my way.

"Wait Mr. Hughes… What the hell are you doing?" I barked. Did he not know cops killed black men for nothing nowadays. In case he seemed to have forgotten, I had a child to live for. His grandson who he and his wife completely abandoned, too, once Trinity so called brought shame to their family's name.

"I want to know what you did with my daughter and my wife?" He asked like I didn't come to his house multiple times asking for Trinity's whereabouts. I saw this nigga was on some bullshit.

"I don't know where you wife or daughter is."

"Sir, are you the owner of this house?" The police officer asked. He looked familiar, and then I recognized him. He was the same police officer that was on Rashawn and Aubrey wedding.

"Yes?" I answered, as I could hear my mom and grandma getting out of the car behind me.

"Okay, we have a warrant to search the house. Mr. Hughes believes you did something to his wife and daughter. He believes you have them held captive here."

"He's fucking lying!" I was beyond frustrated, and looking around all I saw was some trigger-happy cops ready for me to act out to place a bullet in my ass.

"How are you going to have a warrant for my house? This weak ass nigga's wife is probably fucking somebody on his deacon board and Trinity is probably on the run for trying to kill my ex wife in a hit and run. He got yall out here wasting yall time." Now the police officers were staring at Mr. Hughes with confusion.

Trinity was in deed a wanted fugitive.

"I know for sure my wife went with her to turn herself in, but they said she wanted to see Mikey first because she wanted to see her child before she did." He came up with his lie like he rehearsed it a thousand times in his head.

"Mikey, just let them search the house," my mom begged, holding my son in her arm.

"We're going to do that anyway. Hand over the keys," Officer Jenkins said with his hand out. I walked passed him and to my front door. I was over this circus act. I was innocent and trust and believe the Philadelphia police department would be hearing from my lawyers.

"I would think the police department was tired of getting lawsuits," I said, referring to the incident that was all over the news about the police doing a no knock raid that left a little girl with two broken legs.

Opening my front door, the aroma was so foul that I started to gag. Walking inside with the front of my shirt covering my mouth and nose. There was nothing in on the main floor, and I watched the police officers run upstairs. I could hear them opening closets and searching throughout the rooms. My house was completely empty except the furniture.

"Clear!" I heard one of the officers yell.

"Yeah, its clear down here too," another officer confirmed in a defeated tone. That alone brought a smile to my face. I was going to have some fun suing the police department and Trinity'd fuck boy daddy.

"It's not clear. I know yall smell what I smell," Officer Jenkins said, looking over at me. "Check the basement!"

One of the officers yelled back, "There's a lock on the door."

I found that weird. My basement door had a chain locked but not something tat they couldn't unlock themselves. "Come unlock this lock!" Officer Jenkins demanded. I was starting to get an uneasy feeling. I had never put this lock on my basement door. As a matter of fact, this lock wasn't even mine.

"I don't have a key to that lock. I don't know who put that lock on my door, but it's obvious someone been in my house."

"You were just so confident a couple minutes ago." An officer shook his head, walking by with some told, I guess to cut the lock off the door. As soon as the basement door opened, the smell was so strong that I started to empty all of the contents in my stomach. Kai and me had our basement set up like an apartment so whenever family from out of town came over they didn't have to pay for a hotel.

"I see blood!" Officer Jenkins yelled out as he walked down the basement steps. My heart dropped as I brushed passed the other police officers that were standing by the door. Walking into my basement, it looked like something out of horror movies with the amount of blood all over the walls and on Kai's cream carpet.

"Stop! This is a crime scene."

I ignored him and continued to look throughout my basement. By the bar area, I found a decomposing body of what looked like Ms. Hughes with a gun shot wound between her head. She had maggots crawling out of her eye sockets, causing me to throw up again. Going into the family room, I found Sharonda barely body sitting on my sofa along with a fetus sitting next to her. There was a blue barrow of acid sitting in the corner.

"What the fuck?" I mumbled. This wasn't a good look and I knew I was already facing the death penalty.

"The bedroom," I heard and slowly made my way to that area. Tears came into my eyes as I saw a decapitated body of Trinity in the bed. I knew it was her because of the tattoo that was covering the body. I ran to the bathroom ready to empty my guts again. Lifting open the toilet, I was forced to let everything out on the floor. Trinity's damn head was floating in my toilet. Whoever did this was the devil himself. Her face was literally split in two.

"I found a gun," I heard, and all I could do was break down and cry. I knew I was never seeing the daylight again after they locked me up for this.

"Michael Bullock, you're under arrest for the murders of Trinity and Tricia Hughes, Sharonda McDaniel's and her unborn child. You have the right to remain silent. Anything you say can and will be used against you in a court of law. You have the right to an attorney. If you cannot afford an attorney, one will be provided for you," Officer Jenkins read me my rights while placing my hands around my back and cuffing me.

"God give me strength," I silently prayed.

"Mikey!" my mom screamed. I could hear the cries of her and my grandmothers and it caused MJ to scream to the top of his lungs.

"Ma'am, step back, this is now a scene of a murder investigation."

"Mikey, please tell me you didn't do this," Grandma Lucy asked.

"No, I've never murder anyone in my life." I responded with begging eyes for her to believe me. As I was being led to the back of a police cruiser, I saw a Black Challenger riding by with the window rolled down.

Inside, it was none other than that damn Quadir, looking back at me with a wicked grin.

I guess karma was a bitch. I got him arrested and took time away from his child, and now he had me about to spend the rest of my life in prison, away from mine. I guessed Kai had kept her word that he wouldn't kill me, but to me, this was just as bad, because my life was now over.

Epilogue

Mikey

One Year later...

Looking around my cell, I never thought this would be my life. Within two years, I had a baby, lost my wife and got framed for the murders of my baby mother, her mother and her best friend and unborn child. I was facing life with no chance of parole. I couldn't believe Quadir had actually framed me like this, but I guess it was either this or death. Being in jail had me looking back on my past ways and I had a lot of regrets. The main one I had was doing Kai the way I did her. That's why I was writing her this first and last letter.

Dear Kai

I know you're probably wondering why I'm writing you this letter. Our divorce has been over for a whole year. Even though we're divorce I never stop loving you. Regardless of what you think, you will always be my soulmate. Thinking about you and our past life is what gets me through these hard nights in jail. Never did I think I would be spending the rest of my life here, but I guess this is my karma. I'm writing you this letter to apologize. I'm sorry I couldn't give you the one thing that you wanted the most during our marriage. I didn't give you loyalty and stability, as a husband should.

That night with Trinity should have never happened. That was my mistake. Instead of drinking my life away and making bad decisions, I should have been by your side mourning your miscarriage with you. I can finally admit I fail you plenty of times during our marriages. I wasn't the best husband even though you were the best wife a man could ask for.

I'm sorry for not letting you go when everybody could see that our marriage was over. I should have never dragged you through a messy divorce let alone get ya baby father arrested the day you went into labor. I was just angry because with the birth of your child I knew we were over. If I did things right I would have more positive memories with my son, and Trinity going off the deep in would have never happened.

I just want to thank you for loving me unconditionally. Grandma Lucy told me you were now married. Congratulation and I truly mean that. With the past year you had, you deserve all of the happiness that comes your way. I heard ya baby girl looks just a beautiful as her mother. I'm happy for you. I always knew you were going to be a great mother. I'm going to cut this letter short. I just wanted to let you know I love you, and you know me to know I didn't do those horrible things they have me in jail for. But shit happens. Kai, please give me your forgiveness. That's all I truly ever wanted from you. I love and miss you and I learn that loving you is letting you go. Just remember you were my first and only love. Please remember our good times not the bad, and I apologize one last time for all of the harm and pain I cause.

PS. I know this may be a lot to asked but can you please just check on my mom. She's left with my son, and if you ever get a chance tell my son I love him so much and I'm sorry that I fail him as a father.

After writing the letter I knew I would never get a response back, but at least she knew my true feelings. Kai Rose-Bullock would always be my reason to live and now that I didn't have her, I didn't know how much longer I would be here.

Dana Rose

Today was the day that Aubrey and Rashawn were finally going to tie the knot. Hopefully, everything went as planned being as though everybody that was against their union was no longer amongst the living. Yeah, Mama knew everything. I know you hadn't heard much from me throughout my daughters' stories and that was because it was their stories to tell. As a mother, you want nothing more for your children to be happy and find the love of their lives.

Growing up, Kai, Aubrey, and Ava had this fairytale idea of love and marriage. It was mainly because August and me never let them see the bad side of marriage. Love was a lesson to be learned, and I believed my girls had finally found the happiness and love they deserved.

"Baby Girl, you look gorgeous," August smiled down at the beautiful bride to be. Aubrey was a nervous wreck. I guess I would be too if the last time I tried to get married some crazy lady came in with guns blazing.

"Thanks dad."

"What about us Pop-pop?" Kylie said holding her baby cousin Miracle's hand. Miracle was now walking and looking just like her mother.

"My granddaughters are just as beautiful," he professed, picking both of them up.

"Mommy, can you make sure everybody is ready?" Aubrey asked.

"Yes, baby. Now relax! Today is going to be one of the happiest days of your life," I assured her before walking away.

"Everybody ready?" I asked walking into the next room. In this room was all of the groomsman and bridesmaids drinking.

"Yeah. What taking Aubrey so long?" Rashawn asked, giving

me a hug. "You look beautiful, mom?"

"Thanks son in-law. We're about to get this show on the road and they need you out front." I said.

The wedding was about to start, and I needed everybody in their positions. I walked down the aisle with my brother and took my seat in the front. Rita was next, and she walked down the aisle with Anthony. The soulful sounds of Chrisette Michelle was playing, *A Couple of Forevers.* I couldn't even lie this go around was amazing, and everything was even more beautiful. Maybe because with everything that happened it was more genuine. Aubrey and Rashawn came over a lot in a short amount of time. And I was happy they'd finally got it together.

Watching Kai walk down the aisle with Quadir as Aubrey's Matron of Honor. Yes, you read correctly Kai and Quadir tied the knot a couple of months ago in a small destination wedding in the Bora Bora. Miracle was a strong and healthy one year old and Kai was currently pregnant with her second child. It was a boy, and Quadir couldn't have been happier. God worked in mysterious ways. There was times that we thought Kai couldn't even have children and here she was, ready to have baby number two within the next month. I was so happy for my baby girl. I had always considered her the strongest out of all of the girls. Kai had been through hell and back and I love the fact that Quadir was with her every step of the way.

Last month she went through a spout of depression because Mikey had committed suicide in prison. They found him hanging from the top bunk of his cell. What hurt her the most was Mikey's letter apologizing for everything and asking her for his forgiveness. They gave him life in prison with no chance of parole, and I guess that got to him.

Mikey never changed his living will an all of business and life insurance policy money that was over five hundred thousand dollars went to Kai. She didn't want it and turned everything over to his son. She felt bad because the little boy had lost his mother and father. So, she put his money in a trust fund and MJ would be able to get the money when he turned twenty-one.

The business would also be turned over to him at the age of twenty-one. Some people might've thought Kai was crazy and thought she deserved everything Mikey had given her, but Kai heart was of gold. Plus, she was financially set for life due to her and Miracle's multi-million-dollar settlement from the hospital. Right now, Kai was just enjoying being the wife to Quadir Muhammad and a mother to Miracle.

Next walking down the aisle was Ava and Nasir. God knew what he was doing when he put them into each other's life. After all of the craziness with Ava and Amari being kidnapped, Ava took a break from everybody. All her concern was Noah and Noel. Ava had jumped from relationship to relationship and had never gotten a chance to love herself fully and learn to be alone. Nasir was beyond hurt that she didn't want to pick up their relationship, but in all honesty, he had to understand Ava needed to do what was best for her. What she experienced was traumatizing, and she needed time to move forward.

During her time, she landed a job as a psychologist at the Juvenile Detention Center in Philadelphia. Nasir got tired of waiting. He waited damn near a full year before popping up on Ava and demanded that she give him another try. Nasir didn't have to do much convincing because deep down, everything in Ava's life came full circle and the only thing missing was Nasir and Amari. Last week she signed the paperwork to legally adopt Amari.

"Awww," all of the guest cooed. All of the bridesmaids and groomsmen had walk down the aisle, and now it was time for the ring security. Noah, Noel and Amari came strolling down the aisle with headsets, sunglasses and little brief cases. Noah's brief case actually held the wedding rings. Next were the flower girls. Miracle and Kylie walked so gracefully throwing the pedals of flowers. That was until Miracle saw her daddy. This crazy little girl dropped the buckets of rose pedals and ran full speed to Quadir, screaming daddy the whole time.

The music changed and the wedding song started making

everybody aware that Aubrey was about to walk down the aisle. Aubrey was stunning, and my man looked good too, walking beside her. Rashawn actually had tears in his eyes as he watched the love of his life walk down the aisle. As soon as Aubrey reached Rashawn, he lifted her veil and gave her a passionate kiss on the lips.

"Damn, nigga, we didn't get to that part yet," August said, shaking his head like he wasn't standing in front of a damn priest.

"My bad, I couldn't resist," he smiled, looking down an Aubrey who was blushing like a high school girl getting notice by her crush. "Go head Father."

"Thanks... we're gathered here today to celebrate the Union of Rashawn Rogers and Aubrey Rose..." Father Christopher started. The ceremony was breathtaking, especially when they both read their vows to one another. I swear it wasn't a dry eye in the church.

Now, we were currently enjoying ourselves at the reception.

"Here babe," August said handing me a glass of champagne. "We raise some beautiful girls."

"Yes, we did," I agreed as I watched each and every one of them danced the night away with the love of their lives. Their journey to love wasn't an easy one. They we're even put into the positions to look foolish, sometimes down right stupid, but everything were a learning process. Young people nowadays were too ready to give up and not work through the hard times, but I was just happy that my girls found their true loves, just as I'd done, thirty odd years ago.

The End